> **"Michaela, I need a wife."**

"Yes?" Her voice sounded breathier than she would have liked.

"What I need from *you* as my lawyer is a contract," he said. "Grandfather insists that I produce a legitimate heir, but it's got to remain a business arrangement, pure and simple."

"I see." Michaela felt her heart sinking. "It sounds so...I don't know...cold-blooded." Cameron was never one to put emotions first, but this was ridiculous. "Isn't there...someone? Someone you're seeing, who might...want to do this particular deal with you?"

"No one I'd trust," he said. "Unless..." He had a funny look on his face.

"What?"

"Would you consider having my child?"

ABOUT THE AUTHOR

A gypsy at heart, Elda Minger has lived throughout the United States and Europe. She currently enjoys life in Palm Springs, California. When she's not writing, she's usually either gardening, dreaming, fooling around or at the movies.

Books by Elda Minger

HARLEQUIN AMERICAN ROMANCE
117–SEIZE THE FIRE
133–BACHELOR MOTHER
162–BILLION-DOLLAR BABY
229–NOTHING IN COMMON
314–WEDDING OF THE YEAR
338–SPIKE IS MISSING
469–BRIDE FOR A NIGHT
489–DADDY'S LITTLE DIVIDEND

Don't miss any of our special offers. Write to us at the following address for information on our newest releases.

Harlequin Reader Service
P.O. Box 1397, Buffalo, NY 14240
Canadian address: P.O. Box 603,
Fort Erie, Ont. L2A 5X3

Elda Minger

TEDDY BEAR HEIR

Harlequin Books

TORONTO • NEW YORK • LONDON
AMSTERDAM • PARIS • SYDNEY • HAMBURG
STOCKHOLM • ATHENS • TOKYO • MILAN
MADRID • WARSAW • BUDAPEST • AUCKLAND

If you purchased this book without a cover you should be aware that this book is stolen property. It was reported as "unsold and destroyed" to the publisher, and neither the author nor the publisher has received any payment for this "stripped book."

To Henry, my teddy bear,
and the kindest feline I know

ISBN 0-373-16531-5

TEDDY BEAR HEIR

Copyright © 1994 by Elda Minger.

All rights reserved. Except for use in any review, the reproduction or utilization of this work in whole or in part in any form by any electronic, mechanical or other means, now known or hereafter invented, including xerography, photocopying and recording, or in any information storage or retrieval system, is forbidden without the written permission of the publisher, Harlequin Enterprises Limited, 225 Duncan Mill Road, Don Mills, Ontario, Canada M3B 3K9.

All characters in this book have no existence outside the imagination of the author and have no relation whatsoever to anyone bearing the same name or names. They are not even distantly inspired by any individual known or unknown to the author, and all incidents are pure invention.

This edition published by arrangement with Harlequin Enterprises B. V.

® and TM are trademarks of the publisher. Trademarks indicated with ® are registered in the United States Patent and Trademark Office, the Canadian Trade Marks Office and in other countries.

Printed in U.S.A.

Chapter One

"I've heard of spreading one's seed, but you've taken the concept to ridiculous extremes."

Cameron Black sat quietly in the luxurious office as his grandfather continued to expound on one of his least favorite subjects. He'd learned from experience that the best course of resistance was to offer none. Julian Theodore Black could bluster and blow with the best of them, but once he'd vented his temper it would all be finished and Cameron could go his merry way.

"I want a great-grandson!" Julian bellowed now, his face flushed, his white hair and beard offering a startling contrast to his agitated complexion. "I've waited long enough! Damn it, Cameron, what's the point of owning the most successful toy company in the world when I don't have a little one to share it with?"

He offered no reply, and Julian's bushy eyebrows lowered, his expression ominous.

"I've half a mind to rewrite my will and leave you out of it."

That got his attention. His grandfather had never threatened him before. He wasn't sure whether the older man was serious or not, but he decided to jump into the fray.

"I've never wanted to be bothered with a family. You know that."

"Damn it, Cameron—"

"I've been honest with you. You have to admit that."

Julian sighed, then pulled at his full beard, his manner agitated. He looked almost exactly like Kris Kringle, and the image had helped make Teddy's Toys the most respected—and profitable—toy company in the world. Their logo, an adorable masked teddy called Bandit Bear, was as familiar to the world as McDonald's golden arches.

"You've never been in love?" His grandfather was staring at him in a way that made Cameron think the man had never really looked at him before.

"Never. It's a messy business."

"Messy." Julian snorted. "I had fifty-two years of happiness with your grandmother. There's not a day that goes by I don't miss her. Cameron, you don't know what you're talking about."

"It works for me."

"No, it doesn't." Julian sighed, then ran long fingers through his bushy white hair. He was always too busy to cut it, and the staff considered him something of an eccentric old madman. But he understood children, and how they loved to play. He understood the power of imagination. Those qualities had made him a millionaire many times over.

Though Cameron had known he had a job waiting for him when he graduated from Harvard Business School, he hadn't rested on his family name. He was certainly no slouch. Though he had a rather carefree attitude toward his personal life, he loved the business. He'd worked long and hard hours for his grandfather, whom he usually adored.

And he had nothing against children. He'd just never had the desire to marry and start a family. And at the age of thirty-eight, he didn't see that pattern changing.

"It doesn't work, Cameron. And you'd know it, if you had any sense."

Cameron waited, sensing something was about to happen. This argument wasn't following the usual pattern. All his senses were alert, waiting for Julian Black to come to his conclusion.

"You have one month, then I'm rewriting my will and leaving my company to charity. I'm sorry, but I'm cutting you out."

"What?" His incredulity was quiet and intense. Cameron rarely lost his temper, he didn't like the feeling of giving in to any sort of emotion. Now he couldn't quite believe what he was hearing.

"A month and a day," Julian went on, striding out from behind his desk and warming to his idea. "A month and a day in which to find a woman, any woman, make her your wife and, within a reasonable time period not to exceed six months, present me with a pregnancy. Fait accompli. An heir."

"You're mad, old man," Cameron replied, sitting back in his chair. The entire idea was so ludicrous, it had almost made him laugh out loud. Thank God, Julian was joking.

"I'm serious," the older man said quietly. "It's breaking my heart, Cameron, to look at the mess I've helped you make of your life."

This was dangerous territory. Territory he had no desire to explore. He tried for a joke. Anything to lighten the mood.

"Even in those fairy tales you love, the prince is usually given a year and a day."

"I don't have a year. And you, young man, have barely a day. I want some changes, and I want them now."

Cameron stared at his grandfather as if seeing him for the very first time. He had slipped up, badly. He'd had no idea that the concept of great-grandchildren meant so much to Julian Black. When he'd walked into his grandfather's office, he hadn't expected this. Not at all.

First rule of business: know thine opponent.

He'd badly underestimated Julian Black.

"Marriage... and a child," he said quietly.

"Yes." Julian stopped his pacing and stared at his grandson. "Forgive me, Cameron, but I don't see any other way."

"And I'm to love her?"

The question filled the elegant room and emotion hovered between them. Emotion and painful memories.

Julian cleared his throat, and Cameron sensed he was buying himself some time.

"In the best of all possible worlds, my boy, you would. But I don't expect a miracle. A great-grandchild, boy or girl, will be miracle enough for me."

"So you'll have no objections if I basically look for a brood mare." The words were intended to hurt, and he was gratified to see his grandfather wince.

"No. I'm sorry, Cameron—"

But he was already out of his chair and headed toward the door. "Save it. I've got thirty days, remember? Oh, thirty-one, no thirty-*two*, if you count the generous extra day—"

"Cameron!"

His grandfather's voice could still crack like a whip. Years of devoted obedience made him stop with his hand on the doorknob and wait for the old man's last words.

"I want you to keep one thing in mind. In those fairy tales that I so love, a prince setting out on a quest usually finds more than he's originally looking for."

The older man's voice trembled slightly, and Cameron had to fight the urge to go to his side and offer comfort. But he was angry, so angry at this emotional betrayal. He stood his ground and they faced off, two basically arrogant males who were so alike and yet thought so differently on this one issue.

But he no longer had the heart to hurt his grandfather.

"I'll bear that in mind."

MICHAELA LARKIN punched the intercom button on her phone.

"Cassandra?" she asked her secretary.

"Cameron Black on one. I have the feeling it's urgent."

She smiled. With Cameron, it was always urgent.

"Put him through."

"Mike. Hello. I need your legal expertise."

She'd worked for Teddy's Toys before, assisting them in drawing up various legal documents. She'd dealt with both Cameron and his grandfather, Julian. She liked and respected Julian Black.

She'd fallen deeply, soulfully, head-over-heels in love with Cameron the moment she'd met him.

But, unfortunately, her feelings weren't shared.

So she loved him from afar and continued with her usual sporadic pattern of dating. But it did no good, for whenever she spent the evening in any man's company, she secretly compared him to Cameron.

And found her date wanting.

She didn't really go out that much these days; she had her reasons for not wanting to get too close to any man.

But Cameron, that was different. She hadn't been able to resist her attraction to him, and that sensual attraction had been mutual, palpable—until he had jokingly told her he didn't believe in love.

That had squelched all feeling on her side.

Oh, she knew of his reputation. Who in San Francisco didn't? She knew Cameron Black *liked* women enough to let them know the score up-front. She just didn't think she could bear to be one of those women. It would break her heart if she let him love her and then he chose to leave her.

So she simply had her dreams, from afar. And wondered, deep in her heart, if there was a way to make him see reason.

Maybe not reason. Emotion.

Probably not.

He'd started calling her Mike soon after she'd resisted his advances, and she wondered if it was a device he used to help him not think of her as a woman. She was an appendage, a *thing,* a lawyer. She had her uses, but none of them involved the usual activities Cameron participated in with the opposite sex.

"What's up?" She slipped her pumps off and wiggled her toes. Talking with Cameron was a highlight in her day, and she settled back in her comfortable office chair to enjoy herself.

"I need a wife."

She sat up straight. "Excuse me?"

"I need a wife."

She swallowed hard. "I thought that's what you said."

"Look, I know how this must sound. Let me explain." Briefly he told her his situation.

Michaela simply stared at her desk blotter, then closed her eyes and leaned back in her chair again.

"How exactly are you going to go about doing this?" she asked, her voice more breathy than she would have liked. She felt as if someone had just plowed a fist into her stomach.

"With the utmost efficiency. But what I need from you is a legal document that anticipates all the possible pitfalls of this particular relationship, as well as setting absolute boundaries."

Boundaries, she thought. Ah, yes, Cameron knew all about setting boundaries. She felt as if his heart were frozen in ice, and had no idea how to begin to go about reaching him.

Sexual and emotional chemistry was a mystery to her. Why did it hit with one man and not another?

Why did it make her want the one man who was probably the most unattainable?

She brought her attention back to the matter at hand.

"Dinner tonight? Of course I'm available."

Business, Michaela. Business.

They chatted a moment longer, decided on a restaurant, then she hung up the phone and spent the next fifteen minutes staring out her office window overlooking the bay and wondering how she was ever going to endure the thought of the man she secretly loved being married to someone else.

"So, MIKE, the way I see it, I'm basically renting a woman's uterus in exchange for her having carte blanche with my credit cards and spending money to her little heart's content."

Michaela swirled her white wine in her glass and watched the pattern the golden liquid made. She couldn't quite meet Cameron's eyes.

"It sounds so... I don't know... *cold-blooded*, for lack of a better word."

"It's a business arrangement, pure and simple. Don't look so shocked. Marriages have been arranged between men and women since the beginning of time. It's only been a recent experiment in history, the idea of marrying for love."

"Which you don't believe in, anyway." The wine was making her bolder than she usually was with a professional client, and she bit down on her tongue, hard. What Cameron chose to do in the face of his grandfather's ultimatum was really none of her business. None at all.

"I know it may seem rather... *cold* of me, Mike, but the thing is, Jules can't run that company by himself and he knows it. And if he gives it to that disorganized charity he's so fond of, they'll run it into the ground within a year."

She nodded her head, agreeing with him in spite of herself. "I like the guys running the Foundation for Play, but I know what you mean. Bart and Ron aren't the most savvy businessmen in the world."

"That's an understatement."

The restaurant Cameron had selected was quiet and tasteful, with a view that overlooked San Francisco Bay. The menu offered mostly seafood and Northern Italian pasta dishes, and the wine list was excellent.

They'd already ordered, and had finished an appetizer. Now Cameron began to lay out his plan.

"First of all, I want you to know this is not about money."

She nodded her head, reaching for another piece of bread. Cameron's parents had left him an obscene amount of money in their will, and though his fortune didn't rival his grandfather's, he'd invested it wisely and never had to worry about financial matters for the rest of his life.

"I understand."

"I just don't want to see the company that Jules has put his heart and life into go completely down the drain."

She nodded her head.

"He's obsessed with this irrational idea, and it leaves me absolutely no choice but to make this decision."

He'd already explained to her what he was going to do, but she forced herself to ask the next question, anyway.

"Isn't there... someone? Someone you're seeing, who might... want to do this particular deal with you?"

"No one I'd trust."

She watched him as he took another sip of wine. He was a brilliant, complicated man, and she thought of what an utter waste it was that no woman would ever truly share his life.

"I'll need this document as soon as possible. I intend to buy some time on the air and advertise for a woman to fill this position on national television."

She bit her lip. "Won't that...humiliate Julian, just a little?"

"Oh, I have no intention of letting anyone know that he's behind it. I'm going to simply say that the time has come for me to marry, and I'm taking applications." He took another sip of wine, then set down his glass. "Jules will get the point."

"I'm sure he will."

Their main dishes arrived and there was a short silence while they began their dinner. The food was exquisite, the restaurant had a lovely, restful atmosphere, but Michaela felt like she had a hundred-pound weight in her stomach. She forced herself to eat several forkfuls of the pasta she'd ordered.

"How are you feeling toward your grandfather?" she finally asked. She knew she was trespassing, knew that Cameron Black considered himself to be above simple emotions. But she still, with her woman's heart, wanted to try.

"He's guilty."

"Why?"

"Oh, he still feels guilty for leaving me alone with my parents all that time. Not that there was anything wrong with them. They simply liked to have a good time."

A good time, she thought, that hadn't included their little boy. She'd gone to the library and searched through back issues of the *San Francisco Examiner* until she'd found what she was looking for.

The black-and-white picture had been quite revealing. Cameron had been all of five years old, and clutching his grandfather's hand as he'd watched his parents' funeral. They'd been killed instantly when their private plane had gone down en route to Monaco.

He'd been left all alone most of the time before his parents died, with a succession of very efficient nannies. But his grandfather had loved him, brought him back to his enormous estate on Nob Hill. He'd filled his room with toys, and given his grandson everything he could want.

Cameron's childhood had been inextricably entwined with Teddy's Toys, and the public had delighted in seeing the little boy taking his daily walk around the city with his grandfather. Julian Black had been the kind of man who always had candy in his coat pockets or a small stuffed toy up his sleeve.

"And that's why he wants a great-grandchild?"

Cameron sighed, then looked straight at her. And Michaela thought she would never grow tired of studying him, his dark hair, well-defined cheekbones and strong jaw. His eyes were a brilliant dark blue, and so very, very shrewd. And guarded.

"I do realize that family is important. I simply wish I had a younger sister or brother to take up the slack, so I could be left alone."

She took another bite of pasta before she realized the look in his eyes had changed.

"What about you, Mike? Would you change your mind about me and ever consider an arrangement like this?"

"What?" She couldn't believe what she was hearing.

"Would you consider having my child?"

HE WASN'T SURE what had triggered it, but all at once, she dissolved. Her blue eyes filled with tears and she looked carefully down at her almost untouched plate.

"Mike?" he said softly, suddenly unsure of himself.

No answer, but a tear escaped from one of her eyes, then another. She reached up and wiped them away, and it seemed to him that she was angry with herself.

"I'm sorry," she whispered, her voice so low and shaky he had to lean forward to hear her.

"Mike," he said, then took her hand and held it, offering reassurance. She had no idea how she affected him, and that was why he'd struggled to keep their relationship on a strictly business level. The way she affected his senses, and the fact that she deserved more than he would ever be capable of giving her, held him back.

He was, after all, in his own way, an honorable man.

"Mike?"

She took a deep, wavering breath. "I'm sorry. What you said just... brought back memories. I was married before—"

He hadn't known that.

"And we... I mean, *I* couldn't have children. He wanted them quite badly. Children of his own. He wouldn't consider adoption, so we divorced."

The bastard. His reaction to the thought of any man hurting her was so strong it caught him off guard. He tightened his hold on her hand. With his other, he reached into his suit pocket and handed her a clean white handkerchief.

"If you don't want to do this contract, I'll understand."

"No. It's all right. Sometimes it just... catches me off guard."

"How long ago did it happen?"

"Almost five years, since... when I found out I couldn't."

He patted her hand awkwardly, then let go of it while she blew her nose again and wiped her eyes. It was a crime, the way fate masterminded one's life. Here he had no desire for offspring, and the whole choice was being foisted on him by Jules's ultimatum. And, Michaela, sitting across from him, soft and warm and feminine, *excellent* mother material, couldn't have children of her own.

Life was a funny business.

He let her take her time composing herself, and didn't comment when the waiter took away her almost untouched plate. They ordered coffee and *tiramasu*, and sat in silence.

"I can have the contract to your office in three days."

"That would be excellent."

He watched as she took a careful sip of coffee, then looked at him and met his eyes.

"I'm flattered you asked me," she said.

"I was dead serious."

Her eyes were still bright with unshed tears, and it touched him the way she blinked them back.

"You're going to make a beautiful baby," she whispered.

He smiled at her. "You're sure I couldn't interest you in a trial run? What I have in mind for you doesn't have much to do with having babies."

She smiled back, then slowly shook her head.

"I'm out of your league, Cameron. And I think I'm wise enough to know it."

"I could be quite good to you."

She shook her head again, and he watched as her shoulder-length, dark auburn hair swung from side to side. It was straight and smooth and shiny, picking up the low lighting and reflecting it back. He wondered what it would feel like to run his fingers through it, to see it spread out on a pillow beneath her head...

"I know you would be. But I need more than that."

He leaned back in his chair and studied her. "You and Jules, and all that talk about love. It's too bad he's not a little younger, or you older. You would suit each other admirably."

"I care for your grandfather a great deal." He watched as she moistened her lips with the tip of her tongue and wondered why she was nervous. "He helped me tremendously last year, when my father passed away."

"He always goes that extra mile." He hadn't known about that, either. He'd been in Germany for much of the year, checking out new sources of toys for the company.

They finished their meal and left the restaurant. Cameron's car was waiting out front, the driver nonchalantly reading a copy of the *National Star.* When he saw his boss, he leapt to attention and pulled the sleek black car toward the curb.

Cameron helped Michaela into the car, then gave the driver her address.

SHE SAT in her bedroom window for most of the night, looking up at the stars and wondering what her father would have said to her had she told him about this particular problem.

Oh, Pop, what am I going to do?

Michael Larkin had been a policeman, and the best father a little girl could ever want. Fiona Larkin had died in childbirth, but Michael had never made his daughter feel like she was to blame.

It had been the two of them against the world for as long as she could remember. He'd been behind her every whim. Taking her to the local fire station when she'd professed a desire, at the age of five, to be a fireman. Scraping up the money for ballet lessons and coming to every single recital, even though she'd known she was a terrible dancer.

Making her feel loved in a way no one else ever had.

Cheering her on through law school. At her graduation, so proud he was almost bursting with it.

Throwing a party when she passed the bar exams which encompassed almost everyone she had ever known growing up.

Helping her through a divorce that had destroyed her self-confidence as a woman and made her feel as if a piece of her soul had been ripped from her body. By her side, on her side. Always. Fighting for her, caring for her. Loving her.

He'd always been there, until he'd passed away in his sleep almost a year ago. His heart, the doctor had said. He'd always had too much, she thought. And afterward, as life went on in the house she'd grown up in that suddenly seemed so empty without his presence, she'd realized what it meant to be truly alone.

He'd left her the rambling old Victorian house, his cats, no outstanding bills, and enough money so she didn't have to worry about financial matters if she was careful.

She missed him every single day of her life.

As Michaela gazed up at the stars, she realized her father had left her a powerful legacy. He'd taught her what it was to love and be loved. She wasn't afraid of an intimate relationship with a man, and she wanted a marriage, a partnership that encompassed true intimacy and love on every level.

That was why she'd cut Cameron off from the beginning.

Now, the way she felt inside at the thought of him marrying and having a child, she wasn't so sure she'd done the right thing.

Okay, Pop, what would you do?

She thought she saw one of the stars twinkle brightly in the night sky. Funny, how you could be as blasé about religion and an afterlife as you wanted, but when someone you loved died, it was comforting to think of a Heaven. She hoped her father was up there, making people laugh and playing the classical music he loved full blast.

She knew what she had to do. She had to draw up a contract and make sure it met Cameron's specifications. She would have to meet this particular woman, as Cameron would probably bring her to the office to sign the contract and have it witnessed.

She'd have to think of her in his bed, in his arms, making love, having his child... Living a life that, even with that cold-blooded contract, seemed so much more full of passion than her own did, stretched out in front of her. Endless, lonely days.

It wasn't her style to feel sorry for herself, but the facts spoke for themselves. She was honest with the men she dated. Up-front. When things became serious and she thought she could trust them, she told them she would never be able to have a child.

Two men since her husband had left, both gazing at her with a horrible sort of pity in their eyes. Both experiences had been acutely painful. Neither had taken her into his arms and reassured her, told her that it was all right, it was her they loved and not what her body was supposed to effortlessly be able to do.

At least Cameron was more honest about it. Up-front. He wanted what he wanted, and he was willing to go the legal mile to get it. You couldn't fault him for having a devious bone in his body.

Gomez, her father's black-and-white tomcat, jumped up onto her lap. He leaned into her, purring, and she rubbed the top of his head. The cats missed Michael Larkin as much as she did. Though she'd changed a few things in the Victorian, there were three things that remained sacred. Her father's cats, his garden, and his piano.

The tomcat's purring filled the still night air. Michaela pushed her hair out of her eyes, then went back to scratching the cat beneath his chin.

Maybe you should have taken Cameron up on his offer. Maybe, just to feel...something.

Her heart picked up speed at the thought of making love with Cameron. For, despite his deceptively laid-back style, she had a feeling he would be nothing but masculine passion and fire once he had a woman in his arms.

One of the deepest regrets of her life was that she couldn't be that woman.

ONE OF THE deepest regrets of his life was that she couldn't be that woman.

Cameron stood by one of the large windows in his bedroom, a glass of wine in his hand. And wondered at his inability to feel.

Oh, it didn't take a genius to figure out why he was the way he was, why he reacted to things the way he did. He'd never been in therapy, as his personality was one that was deeply private.

He knew that, since he'd been a child, he hadn't trusted in the basic goodness of life. It was so much easier to carve one's way through life, making sure you had absolutely nothing to lose.

Empires could be rebuilt. Companies could be brought out of the red. Business was so easy, because as passionate as he was about his work, there was a part of him that was never touched by it.

He wasn't a man who gave himself over to anything.

Ever.

But love... What was love, anyway? In all of his life, he'd seen it cause nothing but pain. Joy as well, of course, but to his mind there was no amount of earthly ecstasy and happiness that made up for the emotional upheaval that love could produce.

So, he thought as he finished the glass of wine and set it down on the table by the window overlooking San Francisco Bay, you are perfectly justified in what you are about to do.

He knew what Julian was up to. He'd been able to read his grandfather from the time he was small, it was one of the many survival skills he'd honed to perfection during his short but turbulent childhood with his unpredictable parents. Things had stabilized once Julian and Mary had taken him in, but he'd never trusted the world to be a basically good place after his parents had been killed.

He knew this, and was comfortable with his way of looking at the world.

Until Michaela...

He thought of her as Michaela in his mind, though he was always careful to call her Mike. To create a small but necessary distance between them. A distance he'd needed because of the way she'd affected him.

She'd come into his world with the force of a rocket, that first day in the office. He'd glanced up, seen her, and known. Known deep in his soul that this woman was trouble. She could reach him. She could touch him. She brought out feelings in him besides the basically male instinct to get her into his bedroom as quickly as possible.

Oh, he'd tested the limits. Carefully arranged business dinners so he could spend more time around her on the pretext of going over various contracts. Made it a point to interact with her every single time she came into the office. Forced himself to spend time with her, so that he might uncover a flaw, or a reason not to continue this silent fascination.

He hadn't been able to dim the force of his attraction. He hadn't been able to find anything wrong with her, other than a very attractive stubbornness that excited him. For Michaela would be no man's doormat, and would give back as good as she got.

He thought of pouring himself another glass of wine. Ever since agreeing to Julian's ridiculous scheme, he'd had trouble sleeping. He had to find a woman he wanted enough so he would be able to function in their marital bed and produce an offspring that would finally satisfy Julian's quest to ensure he had an emotionally satisfying life.

Well, he'd wanted women. And he'd certainly had them. But he'd never wanted any woman with the complete, emotional intensity he'd felt for Michaela. And she'd made herself as unattainable as a dream.

She wanted love. It was ironic, for that was the one thing that was beyond his power to give. Wealth, luxury, a decadent life-style that most women would sell their respective souls for. But not Michaela.

And it angered him, that she had seen right through to the heart of the conflict between them. And knew him for what he was, a man unable to love.

A man unable to bear another loss.

He sighed, and rubbed the bridge of his nose with his fingers. If she'd agreed to lesser conditions, then she wouldn't be the woman he—cared for.

Loved?

He put the thought out of his mind.

He turned toward his bed, and thought of her there, beneath the covers. Warm and willing and waiting for him. Cameron felt his body's instant response to the fantasy, and wondered at this woman's ability to arouse him even when she wasn't there.

How she might laugh if she knew how foolishly besotted he was over her. How she might use her uniquely feminine power over him if she even suspected she held the smallest portion of his heart.

But that wasn't like Michaela either, and he knew it, was ashamed of himself for even thinking it.

He'd only been half joking when he'd offered her a turn as his wife. He'd been hoping she'd take him up on it. Then, to have to drag the information out of her that she was to remain ever childless. A woman like that, with so much to give...

And here he was, a man essentially dead inside, who was basically going to buy himself a child.

He poured himself another glass of wine, then walked back over to the window and looked out over the sleeping city.

"I know you for what you are," he said softly, then took a sip of the expensive wine. How strange, to be addressing life. And for just a moment, he wished desperately that he were still able to give, to hope, to dream.

To love.

But it wasn't to be. It couldn't be. Cameron Black finished his wine, set down his glass, then turned off the lights and continued to stare out over the sleeping city.

Chapter Two

"This is exactly what I wanted," Cameron said.

"Thank you," Michaela replied as she watched him read the contract carefully. He went over each point, and asked several questions before he was satisfied everything was airtight and ready to go.

"So now?" she asked as she saw him to the door of her office.

"Now," he said, grinning wickedly, "it's show-time."

CAMERON'S info-mercial was a smashing success and the papers picked the story up instantly.

Teddy Bear Heir Seeks Bride! screamed the *Examiner*.

Multimillionaire Cameron Black Decides To Wed! said the *Times*.

Wedding Of The Century! claimed *People* magazine.

It even made some foreign papers, and Teddy's Toys began to be deluged with mail. Each day, bags and bags of letters—thousands of them—were carried up to one of the spare offices by an exhausted mailman.

Mrs. Monahan, Cameron's secretary, was put in charge. Cameron had hired her because she looked and sounded almost exactly like Jane Hathaway on "The Beverly Hillbillies." That, and she was efficient to the extreme.

"I don't know, chief," she said this morning, more than a week after the first info-mercial had aired. "We're knee-deep in mail, and you still haven't found the woman you're looking for."

"I wonder if she even exists," Cameron muttered, then looked up in annoyance as Julian Black popped his head in the door.

"You're a fool, boy!" he called out, waggling one of his fingers at his grandson. "She's probably right here in the city, under your nose, and you haven't even recognized her!"

Cameron glanced at Mrs. Monahan. "Excuse my grandfather for being such an obnoxious romantic." He turned his attention back to his elderly relative.

"If you're so smart, then tell me who you have all picked out for me."

"Now we're talking," Julian said, his bright blue eyes snapping with excitement. He closed the door as he walked into the office, then took off his shoes as he began to wade into the sea of mail. Every so often he picked up a glossy eight-by-ten picture and chortled.

"All this trouble, and she's right under your nose!"

"Get to the point," Cameron said testily. His temper was on a short fuse. He was more than two weeks into his search for a bride, and hadn't found one suitable applicant among the masses.

"That lawyer! You know, Michaela—"

"No."

The silence that followed was loaded with emotion. Mrs. Monahan cleared her throat delicately, then turned to Cameron.

"Chief, why don't I go out and get us some lunch? Is that little Italian deli on the corner acceptable?"

"That would be fine."

Cameron watched his secretary as she waded through the mass of mail and silently exited the spare office. Another reason she'd been hired was that he'd sensed she was a secretary who would be exquisitely sensitive to his many moods. And she was.

"What's wrong with Michaela?" Julian blustered. "She's a beauty, and a thoroughbred. Nice legs, sharp mind, no strain on the eyes, good teeth—"

"Shut up."

Julian stopped midsentence, then simply stared at Cameron, who tried not to meet the older man's eyes.

"You ask her already?"

Cameron said nothing.

"She turn you down?"

"She can't have children." He bit the words out, then wheeled on his grandfather. "I don't want you saying a word about her condition to anyone."

For once, Julian Black was speechless. When he finally replied, Cameron was stunned by the emotion behind his words.

"My God. Poor little girl. I never suspected—"

"She told me the night I took her out to dinner and asked her to draw up the contract."

"That explains the divorce—"

"Bingo. Right again. The bastard dumped her."

Julian shook his shaggy white head, and Cameron sensed his grandfather was off in a world of his own. He tended to tune out that way when he was thinking up a new toy or figuring out ways to manipulate his small family into doing what he wanted them to do.

"I was so sure..." He stumbled on a hill of mail as he started toward the door, and Cameron saw something he hadn't seen before.

Julian was getting old.

It was past time the company should have been turned over to his younger, more capable hands. And it struck Cameron, all of a sudden, that his grandfather was running Teddy's Toys on sheer willpower.

"Jules," he said, his tone softer than the one he usually used when he was fighting with his relative.

"Hmm?" The elderly man turned toward him, but Cameron had a feeling he didn't even know he was there.

"She was my first choice."

He nodded his head.

"Mine, too, my boy. Mine, too." He cleared his throat and suddenly he came back from his mental musings. "A damn shame. I'm truly sorry. I thought... I thought... never mind."

And with that, he turned and left the room.

MICHAELA ARRIVED at the office a few days later, some legal papers in hand.

"Is Cameron Black in?" she asked Mrs. Monahan.

The woman rolled her eyes. "He's in a state today. The deadline's approaching fast, with no one in sight. He's conducting personal interviews all day, and told me not to let anyone disturb him."

"Then perhaps you could give this to him when you see him. It's just a little addendum I thought of that will make the marriage contract even more explicit. I'm sure he'll appreciate it."

"How late can he call you?"

"Until seven. But after that he can reach me at home."

"Excellent."

"Is... is Julian Black in?"

Mrs. Monahan smiled. "He is, but you've come at the wrong time. He takes a nap each day after lunch, and has another forty minutes to go. He doesn't like to be disturbed."

"Of course not, I wouldn't want to wake him. I'll come back later in the week."

JULIAN WASN'T ASLEEP. He was lying on the couch in his office, talking to his wife, Mary. Her picture still graced his desk, and he had only to close his eyes to feel her presence.

"I don't know where I went wrong with the boy, Mary. It was... difficult after you left. I didn't have the touch with him that you did. He went back into himself after you died, and I just haven't been able to reach him."

He sighed, his mind working.

"She was the one, I'll admit it. I saw them together one day in the office, and that's what got me started thinking about babies. Oh, what a child they would have made! Both of them strong and young and healthy. And both so smart. And what a mother she would have been!"

He felt for Michaela. Mary had had trouble bringing children into the world, and they had both wanted a family so very badly. When Cameron's father had been born, it had been the happiest day of their marriage.

"She's an exceptional girl. Her father did right by her, raised a real beauty. Beautiful inside, Mary. You know what I mean. And to think that because of my own selfish desire for a great-grandchild, I caused her to have to tell him something like that. Something that personal. It doesn't bear thinking about."

Maybe he was simply babbling, pretending to talk to his dead wife this way. She hadn't answered him yet, but it comforted him to discuss things with her. After fifty-two years of a good marriage, it was a hard habit to break.

"Oh, Mary, I can't believe I was so wrong. I had that feeling, that same feeling I had when I first laid eyes on you. She came into my office, and I thought, *Here she is. She's the one.* Perfect for Cameron. Just enough fire to stand up to him, but a sweetness there, too. He needs that sweetness. He's scared, Mary, he doesn't even know how much."

He raised his arm and laid it over his eyes, ashamed they were suddenly wet.

"I've never asked for much, Mary," he whispered. "You know that. We worked for everything, and I wouldn't change a single thing about our life together. But now I'm asking you something. A favor. A little one. Well, maybe not so little.

"If you're where I think you are, talk to the man in charge of things. Ask Him if He can do just one last favor for Julian Black."

He rubbed his hands over his face, ashamed he'd manipulated his grandson, ashamed he'd caused a woman like Michaela Larkin such emotional pain.

"I'm asking for a miracle, Mary. I need a miracle, and I don't quite know how to go about getting one. So I need your help, my darling girl."

He wiped his eyes and got up off the couch.

A miracle. Surely it wasn't too much to ask? Julian knew he was in the midst of the last years of his life. And all he wanted, far more than the immense wealth and power his company had amassed, was to know his beloved grandson wouldn't be alone after he died.

FOR OBVIOUS REASONS, those women who lived in San Francisco had a slight advantage in this marital contest. But at the moment, Cameron couldn't for the life of him think what it was.

"So," said the punkette sitting in front of him. "What'ya think?" She snapped her gum and gave him a knowing once-over.

What did he think? Her hair was incredible. Several different shades of red and purple. Her ears were pierced up and down each lobe, but, so she said, she'd thoughtfully taken out the ring she ordinarily wore in her snub little nose.

"I'll let you know..." He checked the name on the application. "Patty. Ah, there are several more ladies waiting outside, but you're certainly... in a class by yourself."

"Thanks!" She flounced up off the chair and swayed out of the room, snapping her gum and throwing him a good-natured wink.

Mother of God, what a day...

He'd seen more than fifty women, one after the other, and not one came even close to the sort of person he'd want to carry his child. How difficult could it be, to locate a sane, well-groomed, intelligent woman who would agree to be his wife long enough to provide him with a baby in exchange for a hefty financial compensatory package?

The articles in the paper had brought every wacko out of the woodwork, and they'd all descended on corporate headquarters today.

Or at least, it seemed that way.

"Send in the next one," he called out the door. Mrs. Monahan was running the interview sessions like a drill sergeant. Five minutes per person, no exceptions.

Cameron was grateful. In fact, in most cases, he didn't need more than five seconds.

He dreaded to see what was going to come through his office door next. And, he reminded himself, these were the best of the applicants, the ones they'd spent days digging in those piles to find.

Some of them looked nothing like their pictures.

"No, wait! Miss, you're not next in line—"

He could hear Mrs. Monahan's exasperated voice just outside the door, then it flew open and a woman pushed her way in. She was easily three hundred and fifty pounds, dressed in a brilliantly colored, tropical print muumuu, and had skin the color of deep, rich, bittersweet chocolate.

"You be Cam the Man?"

"I am."

"I'm Sapphire," she said, sitting down on the couch that graced one wall of the office. "And I'm here to tell you, boy, that I *like* your style."

IT WAS ONE of the longest days of his life.

He almost gave up.

But he wouldn't give Jules the satisfaction.

Then she walked through the door.

Nancy Kilpatrick wasn't exactly what he'd had in mind, but she was young, healthy, and cute in her own way.

The perfect brood mare.

What she lacked in the intellectual department, she more than made up for in charm.

Teddy Bear Heir 37

"I think I'm late," she muttered as she backed into the office. She was juggling a bag of groceries and a plastic cup of cappuccino in one hand, a pile of textbooks in the other.

"Who are you?" he asked from his horizontal position on the couch. His eyes were closed, and he had the beginnings of a migraine.

"Nancy. I had a six o'clock appointment."

"It's seven-thirty."

"I know. I mean, I got on the BART, and I think I must have taken the wrong exit. My sense of direction's lousy, but I just moved to the city and I—"

He sat up, then narrowed his eyes. She'd set her groceries and books down on his desk, and was taking the lid off the coffee cup and attempting to take tiny sips of the hot liquid.

She was of average height, busty and blond. Her eyes were blue and she had freckles across her nose. She looked like one of the milkmaids in a National Dairy Council commercial.

"How old are you?"

"Twenty-two."

"Healthy?"

"As a horse."

"Your mother have trouble giving birth?"

"I'm one of twelve."

"You like babies?"

"I *adore* them."

"You're hired." He lay back down on the couch, then muttered, "Get Mrs. Monahan in here with the contract, and tell me if there's anything about the agreement that bothers you."

"What?"

He opened one eye and looked at her, exhaustion etched in every line of his elegant face.

"Do you want the job or not?"

Her pretty face lit up with excitement.

"Are you serious?"

"Perfectly."

"I can't believe it!"

"Do you mind taking a medical exam?"

"Wow, just like Princess Diana!"

There would certainly be no shortage of stimulation at the dinner table. Though Cameron sensed Nancy wasn't exactly an intellectual giant, she had a vibrancy and an open, sunny disposition that forced him to smile.

"I trust I'll be a little less insensitive than Prince Charles."

"Oh, no, I mean—" A brilliant blush ran up her neck and washed her translucent skin with bright color. "When I saw your picture in the paper, I thought... I mean... you're a pretty sexy guy."

He was sitting up now, watching her.

"So I've been told."

"Chief?" Mrs. Monahan raced into the office. "Did you call me?"

"Yes. I'd like a copy of the contract."

"Oh, that reminds me. Miss Larkin was here, and she delivered an addendum—"

"Let me see it."

Nancy was watching their interplay, blowing on her cappuccino all the while, trying to cool it.

He glanced at her books as Mrs. Monahan rushed out of the room.

"What are you studying?"

"Psychology and human sexuality."

He smiled, and resisted the obvious retort.

"There's something I was kind of wondering about," she said hesitantly.

"Tell me."

"Remember how you said whoever did this would get free rein with your charge cards?"

His smile faltered.

"Yes?"

"Could I...?" She took a deep breath, then let the words out in a rush. "Could I simply have some money to pay my tuition until the end of the semester? Instead of clothes, I mean?"

The smile returned to his face.

"If you give me a child, I'll pay for your entire undergraduate degree and your master's, as well."

She let out the breath she was holding as Mrs. Monahan came back into the room, contract in hand. Cameron smiled down at Nancy, relieved. He'd found the mother of his child at last.

MICHAELA WAS OUT in the garden when the phone rang.

Gomez and Morticia were with her, playing with the leaves on the fledgling tomato plants. There was a corner of the backyard that got quite a bit of sunlight, and Michael Larkin had planted a garden there every year. Now that it was spring, Michaela continued the tradition.

She wiped her dirty hands on the seat of her old pants, then raced for the back stairs and the kitchen. She'd come home a little early this evening, needing the time digging in the dirt to come to grips with her feelings. Cameron might marry another woman, but it would eventually make him happy. As happy as he could be.

She'd needed to come home and garden and feel close to her father. She'd needed to regain her strength.

Now she picked up the phone and was still totally unprepared for the voice on the other end. Or what it told her.

"I've found her."

She closed her eyes, then felt her heart pick up speed. It started to pound, sickeningly fast, as feminine envy shook her to the tips of her toes.

"I'm happy for you, Cameron."

They were some of the hardest words she'd ever had to say.

"About this addendum—"

Quickly she sought refuge in her cool, unemotional, professional demeanor.

"What do you think?"

"It's an excellent suggestion. Could you incorporate it into the agreement immediately? Nancy and I can be by your office tomorrow, late afternoon, so the papers can be signed."

Nancy. Somehow the fact that she had a name made things even worse.

"If it would be more convenient for the two of you, I can meet you at your home. It might be...more private that way." She'd been aware of the media circus from the start, and also knew that Cameron was an intensely private man.

But she also had an ulterior motive. If she didn't have them come to the office to sign the agreement, her colleagues wouldn't have a chance to suspect how this was affecting her.

Coleman, Watts and Burrell was a highly competitive law firm and extremely old-fashioned. The competition between the various legal departments was cutthroat and she didn't want anyone there to know more about her private feelings than was absolutely necessary.

"That's quite thoughtful of you. We'll be staying at the Four Seasons Clift—"

"I know where it is. What time would you like me to be there?"

"Around ten? It's actually more convenient for Nancy this way. She can come to the hotel later because of school, and a medical exam, and several other things she has to take care of."

School. She must be young.

"That would be fine," she said, forcing her voice to remain steady.

She hung up the phone and stared at her dirty hands. Then, not caring about the grime, she put her face in her hands and slowly slid down the kitchen wall.

THE FOUR SEASONS Clift was one of the city's landmark hotels, with a reputation for incredible personal service. Michaela arrived at around nine-thirty, absolutely exhausted. She hadn't slept at all the night before, tossing and turning and wondering if she should have gone ahead and said yes to Cameron's sexual offer.

She'd barely been able to keep her mind on her work. Visions of Nancy had danced through her head, each more exquisite than the last. She had to be stunning, to have caught Cameron's eye. And brilliant. Young.

No cellulite on those thighs.

And a feminine body that functioned with exquisite precision, capable of giving Cameron the child he needed.

Nancy was everything she was not, and it hurt on such a primal, deeply emotional level that Michaela had blocked a good deal of the pain out of her mind.

He'd registered under an assumed name to avoid the press, but had given it to her over the phone late that afternoon. Once it had been confirmed that she was an expected guest, Michaela was shown to a bank of elevators that would take her to Cameron's suite.

He welcomed her inside, a drink in his hand. And it surprised her that he was slightly nervous. She would have thought, with his sophisticated and sensually adventurous life-style, he wouldn't have a worry in the world.

It touched her, seeing him this way. And she didn't want to be touched.

"You've brought the papers?"

She patted her briefcase.

"I cannot thank you enough for being so discreet."

She took the documents out of her briefcase and put them on the desk in the main room, arranging them neatly. Anything not to have to look at his face.

"Would you like something to drink?"

She didn't drink, usually. Now, looking around the elegantly decorated black-and-white suite, she knew she'd have to have something to get through this nightmarish night.

It wasn't every day you got to see your dreams die right before your eyes.

"What are you having?" she asked quietly.

"Scotch."

"I'll have the same."

He seemed surprised, and she wanted to say to him, *Don't be*. One thing Mike Larkin had taught his daughter was how to hold her liquor. She was Irish through and through, and enjoyed a drink now and then.

This one she needed, to make the evening bearable.

They sat side by side on the couch, after he handed her the Scotch. She took a small sip, welcoming the fiery warmth that spread down her tight throat and into her belly.

She wanted to feel something. Anything. And she began watching the clock, hoping Nancy would arrive soon and she'd be able to leave.

She wasn't looking forward to meeting her. Michaela was ashamed of the envy that still filled her. If she was honest with herself, she'd admit she desired Cameron as she had no other man, and it was emotionally devastating to think of him making love to another woman.

She took another sip, wondering if she would ever see Cameron again after tonight. It would be different, with his being a married man. A father. Cameron Black might have led a wild life, but she knew the contract. Once he married, he'd promised, as one of the conditions, to remain faithful.

It was a ruthless document. The woman involved had to agree to a medical examination to make sure all her feminine reproductive parts were in excellent working order. Then she had to agree to wait for an actual, confirmed pregnancy before the marriage would take place.

In exchange, she would be wealthy beyond her wildest dreams.

In exchange, she had to agree to stay home and take care of the child that would be created from this union. The baby.

Cameron's baby.

She set the glass down on the table in front of the couch and pinched the bridge of her nose gently with her fingers. Her breath stung, and for one horrified moment she thought she might cry.

What would he say to her if she turned to him and agreed to spend a night in his bed? After all, he wasn't married yet.

She rejected the idea as soon as she thought of it. That had been the whole point of her not getting involved with Cameron Black. For in giving that part of herself to him, then another part of her soul would die when he left her and moved on to another conquest.

She'd had enough of her soul ripped apart, thank you very much.

"She's late," Cameron said quietly as he refilled her glass.

"I can leave the papers here," she offered, amazed at how steady her voice sounded. "You could call the concierge up to witness her signature."

"Stay for a minute."

His voice was so sensual, so dark and smooth. She wondered what it would sound like in the dark, urging a woman on, whispering erotic words, touching her naked skin with pure, sensual sound...

"The doctor called me this afternoon," Cameron said quietly. "Nancy passed the exam."

She closed her eyes, unable to hide her pain, and heard his soft curse.

"I'm sorry, Mike. I'm just a stupid, bloody, insensitive bastard. I don't know what made me say that."

She forced a smile. "No, it's all right. I've put that all...behind me, now." She reached for her glass and took another sip, bigger this time.

She'd go home, call in sick tomorrow morning, and languish in a bubble bath, maybe work in the garden.

Later she might curl up on the sofa and listen to music. And wonder what she was going to do with the rest of her life.

"Would you mind if I went down to the bar?" Cameron asked her suddenly.

She glanced over at the bottle of Scotch. It was almost empty.

He *was* nervous.

She envied Nancy, having this sort of effect on Cameron. And she remembered the day she'd found out she'd never have a child of her own. She'd doubted, at that moment, that any man would want her. As a wife, lover, longtime companion. Culture could play all sorts of games with male and female roles, but some instincts were too deeply imbedded.

She was flawed, and men could smell it with the keen instincts of an animal.

"Not at all."

This was it. Time to say goodbye. She might see him once in a while, when she did legal work for his company. But it wouldn't be the same. Marriage changed everything, and she had no doubt that Nancy was probably as fertile as a turtle.

"I'll wait for her. Just for a little bit."

Curiosity. It had killed the cat, and it just might kill her. She had to know what Nancy looked like, what the attraction was. She had to see the woman who was going to have everything she'd ever wanted.

"You're a sweetheart."

He was staring at her with the strangest expression, and she held up her hand to ward off the words she knew were coming.

"Don't, Cameron—"

"I wish it could have been different."

"Don't." She turned her head away from him.

He hesitated for a moment, then she heard him get up from the couch. She closed her eyes as hot tears seeped between her lashes.

Then she heard the sound of a door closing.

NANCY STOOD by the huge freestanding map down in the bowels of the BART station. Nervously she chewed a fingernail as she tried to make sense of the map and figure out how to get to the Four Seasons Clift.

She was somewhere in Berkeley, last time she'd asked. She'd gone back up aboveground and had a cup of cappuccino and a chocolate *biscotti* at Caffé Mediterraneum on Telegraph, and bought a paperback psychology book at Cody's with tips on good communicative skills in marriage.

But she still wasn't sure where she was.

A street musician had set up a few feet down from the map and the mournful sound of his saxophone filled the air.

She walked over to him and waited patiently until he finished playing. Then she tossed some change into the basket he'd placed in front of him.

"Do you know which train I should take to get to the Four Seasons—"

He smiled, and she realized he was a little too happy. Drunk, or stoned, or both.

"Be happy, pretty lady. There's a full moon out tonight, and it's time for us to play!"

She walked back to the map and studied it, and started chewing on another nail.

THE SCOTCH had made her tired. And depressed.

Michaela wondered why Cameron hadn't come back yet. And where was Nancy? She returned her empty glass to the bar, and paced the length of the luxurious suite. She'd kicked off her heels while she'd been sitting on the couch, and the carpeting felt good against her bare feet.

Curiosity...

She couldn't resist, and slowly walked down the hall, her stockinged feet soundless on the plush carpeting. She stopped outside the master bedroom, then slowly pushed the door open.

The room was beautiful, the furnishings sumptuous. The covers of the king-size bed had been turned back and a basket of freshly baked cookies was on the bedside table.

Feeling like a thief casing a house for a robbery, she walked over and snitched a cookie.

The rich crumbs melted in her mouth as she wandered around the room, wishing with all her heart that fate had given her a second chance and that Cameron was coming back to her. To be with her.

She walked to the window and stared up into the sky. A full moon floated in the clear night sky, luminous and huge. She couldn't stop looking at it, it positively mesmerized her.

A full moon. A night for lunatics. Or lovers.

She ate the last piece of cookie and studied the moon. She'd stay just a little bit longer, then leave before either Cameron or Nancy returned.

Suddenly she was so very tired, and no longer curious.

CAMERON TOOK a last swallow of his drink and smiled at the cocktail waitress. In the old days he would have had her phone number by now. Hell, he would have talked her into coming up to his room when her shift was over.

Now he suddenly wasn't sure what he wanted.

His grandfather had stunned him with his ultimatum. And strangely enough, in the process of drawing up the contract, he'd felt like he was growing closer to Michaela.

Her husband had been a fool. To have been truly loved by a woman like that, and then to throw it all away? He couldn't conceive of it.

In the deepest part of his soul, he knew Julian Black was right. His entire emotional life was one big bluff, and his grandfather had called him on it. Secretly he sometimes found himself yearning for a closer relationship with a woman, but he still wasn't sure if he was capable of feeling that much.

"One for the road?"

The cocktail waitress was cute, with a curvy figure, red hair and freckles. Suddenly he found that he didn't want to lead her on.

"I'm waiting for my fiancée," he said.

"Oh." She was flustered for a moment, then quickly recovered. "It's a beautiful night to be with someone you love. There's a full moon tonight."

He'd noticed it on the way over, sailing luminous and silver through the night sky.

"So, that's it?" she asked, and he knew what she was asking him.

"Yeah." He filled in his suite number on the bill, and left her a generous tip. He was about to leave when her words stopped him.

"You're that teddy bear guy."

Cautiously he nodded his head. The bar was deserted at this hour, it was clear she was almost at the end of her shift.

"Then you found her."

"Yeah."

"She's a lucky girl."

"Thank you." He hesitated and thought of going back up to the suite and bedding Nancy. He wondered if he was doing the right thing. Then he thought of his grandfather, and how he didn't have that many more years left.

"What the hell," he muttered. "I'll have another one."

JULIAN STOOD next to the huge window in the master bedroom of his Nob Hill estate. He knew his grandson was at an expensive hotel tonight with the woman he had picked to father his child.

He took a sip of his drink and gazed out into the night sky, depressed.

Nothing had gone as he'd thought it would. He'd pushed his grandson into a compromising situation because he'd been too damn proud to go back on his ultimatum.

Mary would have known what to do. He was so godawful clumsy when it came to emotions.

The window was open and the cool, ocean-scented air chilled his pajama-clad body. Turning, he walked back toward his closet, intent on finding one of his silk bathrobes.

He was rummaging in the vast closet when a small box fell off one of the top shelves. He picked it up and almost jammed it back up onto one of the shelves. But something stopped him and he opened it.

Julian smiled. He and his wife had traveled the world in search of toys that would amuse children. Mary had been something of an artist, and he'd encouraged her to sketch various animals. Later he'd sent the pencil drawings to their stuffed animal department, where they had been painstakingly transformed into accurate playthings.

He gazed down at the little pre-Columbian Venus in the box, wadded in among a clump of tissue paper. Mary had found it somewhere in South America, in a tiny shop far off the beaten track. She'd been enchanted with the little statue's swollen, pregnant belly, and had brought it back in the hopes that it might give them more grandchildren.

It hadn't quite worked that way.

But maybe it will tonight...

Julian blinked. For just a moment he could have sworn he'd heard Mary's voice. Carefully, with fingers that trembled, he freed the funny little statue from its tissue paper nest. Then, thoughts of a bathrobe completely forgotten, he took the statue to the large bedroom window and set it on the windowsill.

The moonlight silvered the swollen little belly, and Julian smiled. He could dream, couldn't he? He could hope for a miracle, pray for one.

He didn't quite know how he hoped to accomplish it, but he still wished with all his heart that Michaela could be the mother of his first great-grandchild.

THE SCOTCH made her sleepy, and didn't help her thinking. Usually a single glass wouldn't have affected her this way, but she'd had more than one. And on an empty stomach. She'd been too depressed to eat dinner.

This is ridiculous.

Michaela thought of getting a room—she could afford it—and requesting a wakeup call in time to call in sick for work. She wandered over to the large bed and sat down, trying to collect her thoughts.

You're going to end up one of those little old ladies with her hair in a bun, with a hundred cats and a rocking chair on the front porch.

She laughed at the idea, then bit her lip against the strong flood of emotion.

All alone...

It was a frightening thought. She lay down on the king-size bed and put her head on one of the pillows. She'd rest for just a moment. Ten minutes. Until her head cleared. She took off her suit jacket and draped it over the back of one of the chairs by the bed. Reaching up, she switched off the bedside lamp, and the room was plunged into darkness.

Within seconds, she fell into a dark, dreamless sleep.

Chapter Three

He'd had enough to drink at the downstairs bar that he didn't notice the pair of elegant pumps that had been kicked off in the suite's living room. Nor did he bother to check to see if the legal documents resting on the table had been signed.

Cameron Black was in a foul, highly emotional mood, and was now simply determined to get the matter at hand accomplished.

Impregnation.

Cold and clinical. What Julian wanted. Perhaps it was for the best. Maybe his grandfather was right, pushing him in the direction of a commitment he wasn't sure he would have ever been up to making on his own. Deep in his heart, Cameron had always known he had no desire for a superficial relationship.

Then why have you had so many of them?

He smiled then, a bitter, highly sardonic smile. What foolish dreams he'd had. Boy's dreams. He'd dreamed of a grand passion, a love powerful enough to sweep away all obstacles.

Teddy Bear Heir

The time he'd spent participating in the battle of the sexes had convinced him that such a relationship didn't exist, not for him. The woman who could have conquered the darkness in his soul hadn't been born.

Impregnation.

Something he was probably quite good at. God knows, he'd had more than enough practice. It probably wouldn't take more than a couple of tries, what with Nancy being as healthy and robust as she was.

He hesitated at the door of the master bedroom, placing his hand against the wall to steady himself.

Not too drunk, he decided. *Just enough to get the job done.* He'd surprised himself downstairs, wishing fervently that it could have been any other way. And why had his mind played such tricks with him, continually conjuring up Michaela's image?

A night of sensual pleasure with a desirable woman was one thing. A night in which the objective was to conceive another human life put an entirely different slant on the proceedings. As he'd never attempted to consciously father a child before, the feelings that were flooding him were foreign. Almost frightening.

It shouldn't have to be this way.

But it had to be. Cameron laughed softly, the sound bitter. Damn Julian, but he'd even been right about Michaela. They would have made a good match, but his grandfather's ridiculous demands for a child made their relationship impossible.

Michaela's demands made their relationship impossible. She wanted love, and he'd decided long ago that he didn't have any more left to give. It had all been burned out of him, so long ago.

He didn't have to follow Jules's directive. He knew that. He didn't need the money, and he'd never been afraid of his grandfather. It was just that the old man had done so much for him, given him so much. Was it too much to ask for a great-grandchild?

A small, precious piece of immortality.

Cameron closed his eyes for a moment, suddenly desperately tired. And in the midst of his mental struggles, Michaela's voice came to him clearly.

Doesn't it take a lot of work, Cameron? Keeping it all inside, all that emotion?

She'd asked him that one night, several weeks after they'd met, while working late at the office together. It had shaken him to his very foundation that she'd seen inside to the bankrupt nature of his soul with such utter clarity.

He shook his head to clear it of the memory of her voice. And with sudden ruthless clarity, Cameron knew he was about to do the right thing. For Michaela was the sort of woman who would have probed every last little secret out of him in the name of love. Because she would have cared. He would have never been able to manage their relationship and steer it away from such emotional ground.

Nancy Kilpatrick, fresh-faced and innocent, would pose none of those problems.

Nancy would leave him alone.

Nancy would never touch him as deeply.

Nancy, he could control.

NANCY COULDN'T find the name of the hotel.

"Lady," the cabdriver began again, his tone a study in patience. "How am I supposed to take you to this hotel when you don't know which one it is?"

"It's here somewhere," she muttered, tearing through her knapsack. "I stuck it in this pocket, I know I did—"

"Up to you. The meter's running."

She dumped the contents of her burgundy knapsack all over the seat of the cab, then began scrabbling through the contents. Carefully, each crinkled piece of scrap paper was smoothed out, examined, then tucked away.

Within ten minutes, she admitted defeat.

"Can you call this guy?" the cabbie demanded. "Leave a message at his office?"

Nancy sighed, staring out at the San Francisco skyline.

"I guess I'd better go home and call him in the morning."

HE OPENED the door to the master bedroom and saw the feminine shape outlined in moonlight. And heard regular, deep breathing.

Fast asleep.

He smiled, feeling a certain sort of tenderness toward the girl. He'd decided from the first that he'd be gentle with Nancy, try not to frighten her. He was a man of voracious sexual appetites, and knew she was far more inexperienced. Innocent. Easily embarrassed.

He crossed the room and quietly shut the heavy drapes, plunging the master suite into complete darkness. Then he shed his clothing and stretched out on the bed next to the sleeping girl.

Gently, ever so gently, he stroked her hair.

SHE CAME AWAKE slowly, as if from a deep sleep. He was touching her, stroking her hair, and just that gentle movement, that touch, was enough to heat her blood, set her emotions on fire.

She realized that she'd wanted Cameron Black from the moment she'd first seen him. She'd also known, with a deep, feminine instinct, that he was out of her league. That she would be badly hurt.

Now, having experienced a fair measure of that hurt, she thought of doing something so unlike her, something so deceptive—

You can't...

He grasped the back of her head, his fingers entwined in her hair.

You can't...

She couldn't seem to summon the will to stop him.

I want—

She stopped the thought before it had a chance to fully form, ruthlessly cutting it off. Then she made a move to sit up, to get away from him. Get away from the temptation.

He let go of her instantly.

Both their breathing sounded loud in the silent room. The only sound louder was the pounding of her heart.

Teddy Bear Heir   59

"It's all right." Cameron's voice was soothing and low. Understanding. It brought tears to her eyes.

She would miss him so very much.

"Nothing is going to happen that you don't want," he said softly.

She started to swing her legs off the bed.

"Just let me hold you."

He annihilated her resistance with that one sentence.

She lay back slowly on the bed and he moved to her side, putting his arm around her, letting her rest her cheek on his chest. She remained perfectly still, breathing in his scent, listening to the steady beat of his heart.

Just until Nancy arrives...

How she was going to explain this to either of them was beyond her comprehension. She was already way beyond rational thought. All she knew was that she needed this man, needed his warmth and strength, needed to feel close to someone when she felt so very alone.

They lay that way for a time, until emotion overcame her and she started to cry.

"Oh, no," he whispered. "Oh, no. Don't cry, little one. Don't cry." He patted her back as she sobbed and curled into him.

"Nothing has to happen," he whispered against her ear. "It was a foolish idea, after all."

She sobbed harder, not wanting to make this evening more difficult for everyone concerned than it already was. But she couldn't seem to stop what she'd put in motion.

She could hear deep concern in his voice. "Don't cry. It's nothing that can't be repaired, after all." He cleared his throat. "I'll even subsidize your education until you get on your feet," he whispered, his voice rough with emotion. "I didn't stop to think desperation might have had a hand in your decision."

A gentleman to the end, she thought wearily. A good man, and a kind man.

But a man incapable of love.

Magnetic and persuasive. So very ardent, and loyal to the end. But something had happened along the way that had shut off his belief in his ability to love.

She wondered at his ability to offer her—not her, *Nancy*—reassurance, when he had to be in the midst of some inner turmoil of his own. Michaela sighed, her sobs spent, then realized she was pressed up against him, her fingers touching the naked, hair-roughened skin of his muscular chest.

Naked. He was naked.

So warm, so muscular. So very male.

She curled her fingers into his side so tightly she knew she had to be causing him a certain amount of pain. He didn't say a word, merely let her hold on to him, touch him.

"I'm sorry," she whispered, her voice clogged and nasal. "I'm so very sorry."

"It's all right," he murmured, still rubbing her back through her silk blouse.

There was no excuse for what she did next. Looking back, she might have tried to blame it on the Scotch she'd shared with him, or the fact that she was emotionally exhausted. She might have tried to find some sort of excuse, a weakness, even the fact that she loved him.

She barely knew him.

But she wanted him.

She'd never wanted a man more than she'd wanted Cameron, and the thought of facing the rest of her life and knowing she'd never had the courage to reach out and take what she wanted most of all was intolerable. And unbearably painful.

If she were destined to spend the rest of her life alone and unwanted, she'd take this one night to remember him by. She wanted to make love to this man just once, then slip out the door while it was still dark and never see him again.

He would know. Nancy would know. Together they would figure out someone else had been sleeping in their bed. But they would never realize who it had been. Hadn't almost every woman in America been throwing herself at Cameron? Was it totally inconceivable that one of Cameron's groupies would have found a way into the master suite?

And after their brief time together was over, Cameron and Nancy would have the rest of their lives together, while she would only take this one night. Had Cameron been truly in love with Nancy, or she with him, Michaela knew she would have never contemplated what she was about to do.

But they weren't. And she was. She loved him, she wanted him, she needed just one night with this man of her heart before she consigned herself to the emotional deep-freeze that was to be the remainder of her life.

Still fully clothed, she moved, slid up and over him, pressed herself against him and lowered her mouth to his.

HER FIRST KISS shook him to the bottom of his soul.

Set *fire* to his soul.

Made angels sing.

Completely demolished anything he'd ever thought about women, sex, love and desire.

Shook him, stunned him, woke him up with a vengeance.

She kissed him with desperation in the beginning, then both of them were caught up in a maelstrom of desire, of pure, shimmering sexual heat. They were made for each other, and even if neither fully realized the fact, their bodies acknowledged it with a deep-seated, physical wisdom.

Neither could have turned back even if they'd wanted to.

His hands spanned her waist, and for a moment it surprised him how delicate and vulnerable she seemed. He'd thought Nancy would be more solid, have more substance than this girl who held on to his shoulders and kissed him as if there was no tomorrow.

He couldn't control his response to her, and for a man who prided himself on control above all his other qualities, it frightened him. Aroused him. Seduced him.

He had to follow.

He was lost and he knew it, drowning in her scent, her touch, her lips and tongue, reaching for the buttons on her blouse, unfastening them, pushing the material aside. Cupping the warm flesh of her shoulder, her arm, then her breast. Doing away with the lacy barrier of her bra, then sweeping her clothes off her body and pulling her hard, her naked flesh hot, against him.

He broke that first kiss, then kissed her again. Heard her moan. Before, completely in control, he might have smiled against her mouth, pleased at such a feminine form of surrender. Now he could barely think as he reached for the fastening of her skirt.

He slid it off her. Panty hose and slip met with the same fate, and the whole bundle of clothing was pushed, to the bottom of the king-size bed.

He didn't care if she ever wore clothes again.

All thoughts of taking time with her were forgotten. All thoughts of her virginal fears were swept completely from his consciousness. He'd found his other half, and all his thoughts centered on making them one, as quickly as possible.

He found her wet and hot and aroused. He rolled her onto her back, slid between her legs, then invaded her body with a single, sure thrust.

She answered him silently, eloquently, her body moving with his, her arms tight around his neck, her cheek pressed against his. Then he felt her head fall back, heard her deep, almost agonized breathing.

He tried to prolong it and couldn't. Too quick, too intense, too much. He heard her soft scream, felt her climax. Then he followed her lead.

HE WOKE later in the night, his arm tightly around her. He didn't have to reach for her, as he had no intention of ever letting her go.

Who'd have thought he'd be bowled over by Nancy Kilpatrick? Burn at her touch? The wholesome, freckle-faced, young co-ed he'd met one afternoon in his office had turned into a sensuous, desirable woman that night in his bed.

Life certainly dealt you a surprise every now and then.

He stroked the silky skin of her arm.

They made love again, and this time it was slow and erotic, then sweet and gentle. This time he felt as if he were giving her a part of his soul. And as he fell asleep with his face against her hair, breathing in her scent, he hoped he'd given her a child.

It would be a way of binding her to him.

SHE COULDN'T fall asleep.

The enormity of what she had done couldn't be ignored. What had happened between them had been so powerful, so transcendent, that she felt as if she were Pandora and had just completely changed the world.

He murmured something in his sleep as his arm tightened around her. And though Michaela knew she had to escape and escape now, a part of her wanted to remain with him always.

She found her blouse with her toes, then her lacy slip, moving her foot gingerly over the articles of clothing. At least he hadn't shredded them as he'd undressed her. If she could only manage to get out of the room, she'd be all right. She could finish what she'd set into motion.

Can you?

All through her childhood, her father had told her that actions had consequences. But something had happened to her tonight, something that had made her completely disregard the practical, commonsensical choices she usually made.

Straight A's and impeccable behavior throughout her childhood and adolescence.

A top law student, then passing the bar the first time.

A wild night of lust with an almost stranger in a darkened room, with no identities exchanged but enough heat generated to cause a nuclear meltdown.

Yet she'd never felt more alive.

She remembered...and brushed her thumb over her lips. They trembled. It had been exactly as she'd known it would be, the two of them together.

Well, not exactly.

Nothing had prepared her for what she'd found with Cameron. But she couldn't find it in her heart to regret what she'd done. Except...

Nancy.

The image of Cameron's young bride-to-be finding her in the suite stirred her to action. She found her skirt with her toes, then slowly bent her leg and pulled it up along the length of the large bed until she could grab the piece of clothing with her hand.

Slowly, slowly. The last thing she wanted to do was wake Cameron. What if he decided to turn on the light? She could imagine the look on his face if he discovered who had really been sleeping in his bed.

Her skirt, her bra, her panty hose. Then the silk blouse and lacy slip. She had a moment of absolute panic when she couldn't locate her shoes on the floor of the bedroom, then remembered she'd kicked them off out in the front room.

The darkness in the suite gave her absolutely no sense of time. Hours could have passed. Or mere minutes. The only thing she knew was that she had to get out of this bedroom without waking Cameron.

Was he a light sleeper? Yet another thing she didn't know about the man. She'd only given in to him in the most primal, intimate way possible, exposing every single sexual secret her body had to offer. But she didn't know if he was a light sleeper or not. Or even how he usually took his morning cup of coffee.

The only thing she knew with total certainty was that he was a first-class lover, an extraordinarily gifted individual between the sheets.

This bothered her.

Michaela sensed that even if he'd ever participated in a conventional courtship, there would be many things a woman would never find out about this man.

Teddy Bear Heir 67

Cameron was intensely private. It was just the way he was.

For just an instant her heart went out to Nancy.

Then she continued her escape with renewed effort. Her clothes wadded into a large ball, she worked on gingerly extricating herself from beneath his muscular arm.

He murmured in his sleep.

She froze.

He pulled her more tightly against his side and kissed her beneath her left ear.

She bit her lip in frustration.

Then he stretched in his sleep and, instead of watching the muscular play in that magnificent male body, she waited for the exact moment when his hold on her lessened, and slipped from beneath his grasp. Then she backed away from the large bed, her bare feet making absolutely no sound on the thick carpeting.

Cameron rolled over onto his stomach and buried his face in one of the pillows. Silently, with as little wasted motion as possible, Michaela dressed, grabbed the jacket to her suit, which was still draped over the chair, and slipped out of the master suite.

She stopped only long enough to grab her pumps, her briefcase, and her purse, then she was out the door.

NANCY FOUND the elusive piece of paper with the hotel's name on it when she reached the apartment she shared with two other girls. For some reason she'd stuck it on top of her dresser, not in her knapsack. Now, though it was almost dawn, she figured she owed Cameron Black an explanation as to why she hadn't bothered to show up.

After all, it wasn't every day that a girl got to marry a millionaire. She certainly didn't want him to think she was blasé about the whole thing.

Now that the moment of truth was at hand and she was actually about to move in with San Francisco's most infamous playboy, she found she needed some of her familiar things around her. She packed a small suitcase, then two boxes. At the last minute she stuck the paperback full of marital tips into her knapsack.

Then, calling the limousine service that Cameron had suggested she use in the first place, and most certainly bill to him, she sat down and waited for the driver to arrive.

This time she'd leave all directional details in someone else's capable hands. That way she had at least a small chance of reaching her destination.

MICHAELA CHECKED into the same hotel once she reached the registration desk. She knew how she had to look in the clerk's eyes, and she didn't even care. Her makeup was smeared, her panty hose balled into a wad of material in her purse. But as long as she had the plastic to support a night in a hotel like this one, why should it bother her what the young man in the front lobby thought?

She had enough to worry about, like how to repair the shambles she'd made of her life.

She'd made cursory attempts to repair her makeup on the elevator ride down, but now, key in hand and the necessary forms filled out, she went back up the elevator, stopping at a different floor from Cameron Black's, and let herself inside one of the elegant rooms. Then she did exactly three things.

She locked the door behind her.

She undressed down to her slip.

She fell into bed and didn't even notice her head hitting the pillow.

NANCY WAS superstitious.

On the eve of embarking on her relationship with Cameron Black, she knew she had to make sure things went as smoothly as possible. And she'd need a little more help than a few marital tips, or even marital aids.

Thus, on her left pinkie finger she wore the good-luck garnet ring her grandmother had given her, rinsed her face exactly fifteen times before blotting it dry with one of the hotel's plush towels, and spritzed herself with her favorite cologne before exiting the lavish bathroom.

Cameron was asleep in bed, his face pressed into the pillow. Naked. And really quite magnificent.

She studied him silently and wondered at what she had agreed to do. She didn't feel a tremendous amount of guilt. Her older sister had been a surrogate mother for her closest friend, and Nancy saw this arrangement she'd agreed to as something quite similar.

Looking at Cameron, she knew she could grow to love him. He scared her, just a little. But she sensed that beneath his powerful front, there was a basically decent man.

She'd researched him at her school library, and had decided she was never going to take advantage of him. Being filthy rich made for some complications in life, and she was absolutely certain she wasn't going to be one of them.

Her gaze flitted over his strongly muscled back, down to his buttocks, then skimmed his legs and finally ended at his feet.

He even had sexy feet.

Nervous, she darted back into the bathroom. Nancy carefully brushed and braided her blond hair, then put her pink chenille bathrobe on over the lacy pink nightgown she wore. She pulled on light pink kneesocks with white polka dots, then turned off the bathroom light and went back into the darkened bedroom.

What a night.

She'd watched the sky lighten into pale gold and pink as the limousine had raced toward the hotel, watched the full moon fade slowly against the morning sky. Now, as she lay down in the large bed next to her future husband, she closed her eyes and said a small, heartfelt prayer, hoping that everything would work out for the best for everyone concerned.

Exhausted from her night of misdirection, she finally fell into a light, nervous sleep.

Chapter Four

The following morning, Julian Black woke up, stretched, then walked to the window and picked up the little pre-Columbian Venus. Rubbing the statue's swollen belly thoughtfully, he set it back down on the windowsill.

Michaela roused herself out of a deep sleep when her wake-up call jarred her awake, then put in a call to her law firm. She hadn't taken a sick day so far this year, and now seemed as good a time as any. After making the necessary excuse as to why she couldn't come in, she hung up the phone, pulled the covers over her head and went back to sleep.

And Cameron Black woke up and looked at the woman who had made him lose all rational control. The woman who had turned him into a raging sexual *animal*, totally driven by a naked, insatiable libido.

The woman who was now tightly curled up on her side of the king-size bed and wrapped in a bright pink chenille bathrobe.

But it was the polka dot socks peeping out from beneath the robe's hem that stunned him.

HE DIDN'T want to push Nancy, not this first day.

But he was beginning to understand the roots of sexual obsession. *Fatal Attraction, Basic Instinct, Damage* had all been merely movies before last night, but now—

They'd practically burned down the bedroom, the sexual heat between them had been that intense. Yet he knew she was a shy, modest girl, so Cameron decided to make absolutely no reference to how thrilled he was at their incredible sexual compatibility.

That resolution lasted until the end of breakfast.

She was sipping a cup of cappuccino and he was having his usual cup of morning coffee—black, as was his preference—when he made an oblique reference to the previous night.

She blushed a furious rose and averted her eyes.

"We didn't... we didn't sleep together last night," she whispered. "I mean, we slept together but we didn't—" She halted. "You know, sleep together."

He started to protest, then took a good look at how young she was. They were breakfasting out on the balcony, the early spring San Francisco morning was mild. Nancy looked so fragile, he simply didn't have the heart to insist she was lying.

It would be like kicking Bambi.

"Well," he said, trying to figure out what to say next. "Well." He remembered the deal they had made, and how carefully he'd spelled out the terms of their agreement. Nancy, with the help of her gynecologist, had figured out her most fertile times of the month, and he'd agreed to confine himself to approaching her bed at those times. Thus, according to her cycle, he wouldn't be sleeping with her for another few weeks.

Last night had been the perfect time for conception.

Last night had been perfect, period.

Now, his sperm count depleted and her particular cycle finished, optimal conditions for pregnancy no longer existed. But perhaps, just perhaps, Nancy was a lusty lass who liked to fool around and would consider breaking their agreement.

Perhaps Nancy had liked what had happened in their bed last night. Perhaps he could persuade her...

"Nancy," he said softly. "About last night—"

"Nothing happened," she said, and this time he saw a desperate sheen of tears in her eyes. She stood, and, taking her cup of cappuccino, went back inside into the master suite and locked herself in the bathroom.

MICHAELA SLEPT until seven that evening, then soaked in a tub filled with rose-scented bubbles. She wanted to eradicate all traces of Cameron's scent from her body.

Too bad there wasn't a bubble bath for the brain.

Thus, here she was, considered by many an incredibly talented lawyer, a single woman extraordinaire, a woman on top of the world in this brave new world of modern dating and interaction between the sexes.

Here she was, miserable.

She had every reason to feel lower than an earthworm, and she did. What she had chosen to do last night was absolutely inexcusable. But why couldn't the gods have been kinder?

Why couldn't Cameron Black have been lousy between the sheets? Why hadn't he had bad breath or cold, sweaty, clammy hands, or kept a pair of short black socks on his feet the entire time they were doing the dirty deed?

The room was totally dark, you moron, she answered herself. *You wouldn't have seen the socks.*

Okay. Fine. Why hadn't he touched her in all the wrong places? Or why hadn't he rubbed her with the pressure and intensity of the machine one of the hotel workers had been buffing the floors with early this morning, so she would've been sexually numb by the end of their lovemaking and would've had a reason for wanting to never be caught dead in bed with the man again?

Or snorted when he laughed?

Or wheezed after sex or developed a crick in his back? Or told old war stories or bad jokes far into the night? Or—

The imaginary list was endless, but it was useless. Cameron was exquisitely sensitive to the female body and perhaps—

She tried to stop the thought, it was just too depressing.

Perhaps it was like that with him and every member of the fairer sex. Perhaps what happened last night was the normal drill, so to speak, for the sexually brilliant Cameron Black.

Teddy Bear Heir 75

No wonder he'd had any woman he wanted. The only thing that puzzled her was how his fame hadn't spread to Europe and beyond.

That was depressing. Cameron plus any woman equals a white-hot combustion. A sexual meltdown. A chemistry so intense she could barely breathe, and she was lying in a bathtub full of bubbles just *remembering* what had happened, for God's sake!

She tried to blank her mind and found she couldn't. She kept remembering sounds and sighs and smells, touches and soft moans, deep breathing, strong hands, a sure touch, a slow hand—

Determined to forget, Michaela pulled the plug with her toes, then stood in the bathtub, slid the glass door shut and turned on the cold water.

Full blast.

IT WAS HARDER to forget than she thought.

Five days after *L'affaire de l'hôtel*, or *L'affaire de le Stoopid*, as she preferred to refer to it, Michaela found herself in Cameron's office, going over yet another business contract.

"Are there any loopholes?" Cameron demanded. "Any way that they can back out of the merger once they've signed?"

She'd gone over the contract countless times, as both Cameron and Julian were ruthless negotiators. You didn't get to be a millionaire by being Kris Kringle, even if you did own the biggest and most successful toy company in the world.

"None. It's airtight."

"Good."

She was gathering papers into her briefcase when he gestured her to sit. Cameron had always had a sort of natural arrogance that she actually found quite appealing, but now everything he did set her nerves on edge. She wondered what he was going to do.

"Can I ask you something?"

She nodded her head.

Then the miraculous occurred. Cameron Black, San Francisco's answer to The Sheik, actually blushed.

Blushed!

She stared at the dark color slowly seeping up his neck and into his face.

She swallowed. Licked her lips. Dug her nails into her palms.

This is it. He knows. Talk about unprofessional business behavior—

"It's rather... personal," he said quietly.

Oh, like personal matters when you've had my legs up over your shoulders—

"Mike, why would a woman want to totally forget an incredible sexual experience?"

For one awful moment the office went totally still, then darkened. The air seemed heavy, too heavy, it hurt to draw air into her lungs. She thought she was going to pass out from total shame until she took one quick peek at his face and realized he had no idea what had happened that night.

None at all.

Zip.

Nada.

Michaela took a deep breath and felt a measure of sanity return.

"Why, whatever do you mean?" she replied.

"It's just... we had this agreement, but..."

She was one sick cookie, because she encouraged him.

"You can tell me, Cameron. I won't tell anyone. I'll consider this a... a business conference, and therefore confidential."

The road to hell in a handbasket was paved with banana peels. *Actions have consequences. What are you doing?*

"I don't suppose it's any news to you that I came to this... marital arrangement with a considerable amount of sexual experience."

"Mmm." She nodded her head and tried desperately to curb the images flitting through her brain.

"I thought I would take things slowly with Nancy, perhaps even wait until her next... fertile period." He shot her an intense look. "Is this bothering you, Mike?"

Oh, not in the way you think...

"Not at all."

"But that night—"

"Yes?" She couldn't help herself, it was a compulsion. She had to know if what had happened in that hotel room had shaken him, emotionally devastated him, sexually enthralled him, as much as it had her.

"I— Well, she— I thought for a moment that we weren't going to go through with the... sexual arrangement, after all."

"Mmm." She nodded her head again, trying to radiate calm and understanding.

Mother Teresa, that's me.

"But—and this is the part that I don't quite understand—she . . . she—" He glanced at the door. "This goes no farther than this office, is that understood?"

"Absolutely." *Boy, you've got my word on that.*

"She turned into . . . this voracious sexual animal—"

Why, thank you.

"And I can honestly say that in all my experience with women—"

Go on, go on.

"I just— I've never—"

That sexy blush suffused his face again, and Michaela had to bite her lip to keep from shouting with joy.

Yes! It wasn't Cameron plus any willing female, it was something between the two of them!

She came back to earth rather quickly when she realized that, no matter how resplendent the experience had been, it could never be repeated.

She cleared her throat.

"I understand, Cameron." *Good, that's very good. Keep the voice soft and soothing, the expression concerned.*

"But now, there seems to be a problem."

Uh-oh.

"She doesn't— She claims that—"

Michaela swallowed quickly, willed her throat to open back up, and determined to tell one last little white lie. For Nancy's sake.

"The two of you never had sex."

"Yes!" He looked at her with such amazement in his expression that she had to dig her nails into her palms to prevent herself from falling down at his feet, groveling, humiliating herself completely and confessing to the entire thing.

"Mike? You don't look well. Is something wrong?"

The perfect opening in which to confess all—and, of course, she chose not to take it.

"No, I'm okay, I think it must have been something I ate at lunch. But about Nancy—"

"I'd appreciate your help with this matter."

"I understand. You see, when a woman first starts to have sex on a regular basis, she goes kind of crazy. Considering the sorts of men out there who typically initiate her into the act, this is understandable. But when it happens and perhaps the woman is feeling a little guilty about it and then it turns out to be an absolutely transcendent experience—"

Calling Dr. Freud to the lingerie department...

"I can see how a little denial might be in order."

She studied the look on his face and realized she'd completely snowed him. Cameron Black might be a whiz in both the bedroom and the boardroom, but he had absolutely no idea what made a woman tick.

How nice. At least he's normal in that respect.

"Hmm." He leaned forward and steepled his fingers. "You know, it makes sense."

I'm glad one of us thinks so...

She smiled, then stood. "Well, I hate to counsel and run, but I do have other appointments today."

"Of course. I'll walk you to the elevator."

It took every ounce of willpower she possessed not to throw herself into his arms as they walked down the hall together.

HE WOKE UP in a sweat, and glanced toward the door of his bedroom.

Cameron knew that beyond that doorway lay the hall, and beyond that lay the door to Nancy's bedroom. She was probably asleep, lying beneath the covers and looking absolutely adorable in one of her fluffy little nightgowns.

It was the damnedest thing. Normally, Nancy wasn't the type he usually went for. His sexual type leaned much more toward Michaela, tall and leggy brunettes or redheads.

He'd never really had a thing for blondes.

Knowing that the woman he desired more than any other lay only a few rooms away was doing terrible things to his libido. It was sheer, unmitigated torture.

How could she have forgotten so easily?

He hadn't demanded an accounting of Nancy's sexual experience or lack of it, but she had volunteered the fact that she was still a virgin. It astounded him, that such an innocent woman with such a lack of experience could have led him to such sensual heights merely two weeks ago.

But that means in roughly two more weeks...

He lay back in bed, his head beneath his hands. At first he'd thought Nancy might wish to come to his bed of her own volition. He'd left the door open, and a lamp on at one end of the massive bedroom.

He didn't want to be subtle, he wanted to have some of the greatest sex he'd ever had in his life. Again.

But she hadn't approached him. Their contract had stipulated that they could continue to live largely separate lives, so she went to school and he went to work and the few meals they shared were quietly miserable.

She seemed ashamed, and that made Michaela's theory seem even more valid.

Rolling over in bed, Cameron punched his pillow and lay down, determined to sleep. But he knew it was going to be another long, lonely night.

And in a brief, petty moment, he wondered why the woman he'd had the most incredible sex of his life with couldn't be going through the same total hell he was experiencing.

SHE WAS. Oh, she was.

Michaela glared at the luminous numbers on the clock by her bed—4:18 a.m.

Four-eighteen in the morning and all she could think of was Cameron.

This whole thing was getting out of control. She'd resolved, after that one session of pseudo counseling in his office, that she was never, ever, *ever* going to do anything as dumb again. *L'affaire de Freud* had joined *L'affaire de le Stoopid,* they were both right up there at the top of life's most regrettable moments.

He'd called her at her office one more time about Nancy. And Michaela had absolved part of her guilt by telling him to take time, to be tender with her, to buy her little presents and delight her, to listen to her worries and her thoughts about school.

To even take her away for a romantic weekend. Paris. Rome. London.

To simply be there for her.

Hell, by the time they finally got back into bed with each other, they'd probably *be* in love. And the power of suggestion was a wonderful thing. Cameron would almost certainly think he was having wonderful sex, he'd be so worked up after almost a month of celibacy.

And that would be that. And she would quietly quit the law firm, enter a convent and get on with her life...

She rolled over in bed, disturbing both Gomez and Morticia, then punched her pillow and lay back down among the covers, determined to sleep.

Instead, she watched the sun rise.

"YOU LOOK terrible, Mike."

"You know, I don't feel so good."

They were sitting in a little French bistro having lunch. Michaela had just completed another complicated contract for Teddy's Toys, and Cameron had insisted on taking her out to lunch.

He seemed all smiles today, and Michaela could guess the reason.

Nancy's fertile period was coming up. Within days. And Cameron looked like life was treating him well, indeed.

He looked heartbreakingly beautiful to her on that Thursday afternoon. They were sitting by the large front window of the restaurant, and bright spring sunshine made his dark hair shine. His brilliant blue eyes seemed so alive, and her fingers ached to touch the slight cleft in his chin.

They'd just finished their soup when he confided in her.

"Your advice made a great deal of difference. I think Nancy is enjoying our arrangement a lot more these days."

This is my penance for what I've done, Michaela thought. *To listen to Cameron and realize how happy he is with Nancy. And that's as it should be, for she can give him the child he wants to have.* Her father had raised her within the strictures of the Catholic church, and guilt was her constant companion.

But if their relationship was going well, then that was what was important, wasn't it? She'd stumbled and fallen once, gotten back up and dusted herself off. Surely she could forgive herself. They could all move forward from this time. She would never confide in anyone about what had happened.

She'd thought of going to confession during one of her blacker moments, then realized the priest would probably have a coronary. Besides, she knew him, he knew his congregation, and she had no desire to share this particular sexual fiasco with anyone but her conscience.

A chicken dish followed the soup, then an exquisite apple tart and dark French roast coffee. They walked back to the office, and had almost reached it when Michaela became dizzy.

She clutched at Cameron as she stumbled, and would have fallen if he hadn't been alert and caught her. With strong, sure hands, he guided her to the curb, where he eased her down and pushed her head between her knees.

"Just breathe," he whispered, stroking her back in a comforting manner.

She did, and as her vision cleared she laughed self-consciously. "That was pretty stupid," she muttered.

His blue eyes were shrewd. "How long has it been since you've seen a doctor?"

"I'm healthy as a horse. I never go to doctors."

"You seemed kind of... I don't know. Queasy. In the restaurant, when we first walked in."

"That fish—it was such a strong smell."

"I think I've been working you too hard."

"Oh, no." She struggled to her feet, and he insisted on giving her his arm. It was the sweetest sort of torture, being allowed to touch him.

"You should take a few days off. A long weekend."

How could she explain to him that the law firm of Coleman, Watts and Burrell frowned on personal days, personal emotions, even the concept of a personal *life*. More than once, Michaela had found herself wishing she had something along the lines of a wife. The male members of the firm had the luxury of having partners who kept the home fires burning.

She had Gomez, Morticia and a whole two rows of tomato plants.

Oh, stop feeling sorry for yourself. Now.

By the time they reached the office, they were laughing.

JULIAN BLACK gazed down at the couple on the sidewalk below from his office window on the fifth floor. Absently his finger rubbed the little statue's belly. He'd brought her to the office, and even though he knew it was almost hopeless to wish for a miracle, he kept dreaming.

He liked Nancy Kilpatrick. A lot. There was something very sunny and uncomplicated about the girl. She was emotionally whole, and a hard worker.

But he wanted Michaela for his grandson.

He'd frowned in concern when he'd seen Michaela stagger and almost fall, then seen the concern in the way Cameron escorted her to the curb. The way he cared for her.

Oh, he could have put the entire matter down to his grandson's upbringing. Mary had made sure Cameron possessed an excellent set of manners, and they were reinforced daily by the expected behavior of both employer and employee at Teddy's Toys.

But it was more than that.

He'd watched them together in the office long before he'd issued the ultimatum he'd come to regret.

I was so very sure...

He continued to watch them until they entered the building, then turned away from the window with a deep sigh.

TONIGHT was the night.

Cameron couldn't remember a night he'd ever felt better. He'd played racketball at the club this morning, then put in a solid day's work. Mrs. Monahan had sent flowers to the house this morning, several bouquets of the daisies Nancy loved. And his ever-efficient secretary had also made reservations at one of the most romantic restaurants in the city.

Dinner had been quite pleasant. But something wasn't quite right.

Nancy seemed scared.

Now, lying in the large bed in the master suite, Cameron listened as the water in the bathroom was abruptly turned off. He held his breath as the door opened, then Nancy was illuminated in the doorway, dressed in a peach satin nightgown.

She looked absolutely darling.

He held out his hand, trying to encourage her, hoping to quell her obvious fears. Well, she'd been a virgin when she'd come to his bed, and their wild night of sex had almost frightened *him*, it had been that intense. So what did he expect?

"Don't be afraid of me," he whispered. "I don't think I could bear it."

He was rewarded by her shaky smile.

She'd left her long blond hair loose, as he'd requested, and he liked the fact that she willingly obeyed him. It made things so much easier. As she sat down on the bed next to him and looked down at him, he slowly sat up, took her face in his hands, and gently kissed her.

And nothing happened.

Puzzled, he looked at her upturned face. Her eyes were closed, her lips moist. When she opened those blue eyes, they weren't hazy with passion.

They were miserable.

He wasn't going to accept defeat.

Careful not to frighten her, he kissed her again and tried to remember the feeling of her sliding on top of him, that electric sensation when their lips had first met.

Nothing.

Her lips were trembling, her hands were cold. He felt like hugging her, comforting her, but not having a wild, sexual, no-holds-barred night with her.

"Nancy?"

She looked up at him, her expression one of abject misery.

He sighed. It was impossible. It was incredible. She'd been telling him the truth all along, and he'd been far too insensitive and caught up in his own thoughts to believe her.

"Nancy," he said softly. "I'm not going to be angry with you, and this time I might even actually listen." He moved away from her, opened the bottle of expensive wine he'd had chilling by the bed. "Why don't you tell me exactly what happened that night?"

Slowly, haltingly, she told him her story. After his first glass of wine, Cameron was vaguely amused. By his third, he was furious. But he was nothing but supportive with Nancy, even when he escorted her back to her bedroom and told her they would talk more in the morning.

He assured her none of this was her fault, and that life would continue along much the same lines it had before this little revelation. Except that she would no longer be expected to have sexual relations with him, for the time being. At least until they got this thing sorted out.

Back in the privacy of his master bedroom, Cameron poured himself another glass of wine and stood on the balcony that overlooked the lights of the city.

He took a sip of wine and set the delicate stemmed glass down on the small table outside.

"If I didn't sleep with Nancy," he said to no one in particular, addressing the night and the stars above, even the full moon riding high in the sky, "then who the hell *did* I sleep with?"

IN THE bedroom of her Victorian house, in quite a different neighborhood of the city from Cameron, Michaela slept blissfully, the sleep of the truly exhausted.

And had no idea her world was about to be totally turned upside down.

Chapter Five

The entire office was in an uproar when Michaela arrived with the latest contract.

"What's going on?" she asked Mrs. Monahan, whose body language gave the expression "running around like a chicken with its head cut off" a whole new meaning.

"It's chief," she whispered. "I've never seen him like this."

Michaela indicated the thick sheaf of legal papers in her hand. "Should I talk to Julian about this particular contract? Kind of bypass Cameron for today?"

Mrs. Monahan rolled her eyes, looking for all the world like one of those horses racing out of a burning barn in a late-night Western.

"That might be wise."

CAMERON was in his office, deep in thought.

Somehow, some way, he had to reach this mystery woman. He'd spent the past few weeks since his disastrous night with Nancy, thinking of exactly how he was going to accomplish this.

It was a peculiar thing, what incredible, incendiary sex did to a man. Now, the thought of having a child was the furthest thing from his mind. The thought of continuing to oversee the empire known as Teddy's Toys held very little appeal, as well.

The thought of finding this woman, tracking her down, and spending a few weeks in bed with her was uppermost in his mind.

But where to begin?

Well, this was the age of information, and television was still the most powerful medium known to mankind. The first info-mercial had worked and brought women into his life in droves. He'd have to make another one, and ensure that it did the job.

It would have to be subtle. A masterpiece of production. He couldn't just get on national television and ask who had been sleeping in his bed. Half the female population of San Francisco would probably show up. And he was only interested in one of them.

He called in the same writer who had created the first info-mercial, and tried to explain exactly what he had in mind. And why.

Chuck Berrigan was in his early fifties, fat, slovenly and unshaven. He constantly had an expensive Cuban cigar hanging out of his mouth, and looked like a character in a Billy Wilder comedy. He had a fondness for khaki pants and baggy sweaters, and wore his gray hair long enough to brush his collar.

But he had the heart of a pussycat beneath his brusque demeanor, and wrote copy like no one else.

Teddy Bear Heir

Teddy's Toys had employed him before, and he'd written several of their most successful ad campaigns, including the famous one three Christmases ago in which Julian had dressed up as Kris Kringle and Mrs. Monahan had had to suffer through the same photo session dressed as a long-suffering elf. But the reindeer they'd rented for the day had loved her and practically licked the skin off her forearms.

Chuck was pacing the length of the office, back and forth, back and forth. His cigar remained unlit, as Cameron had no fondness for secondhand smoke. Finally the writer stopped pacing and faced his employer.

"Let me get this straight," he said. "You went to bed with this broad and don't even remember who she was?"

"The room was totally dark," Cameron explained patiently. He couldn't blame Chuck for his reaction. The whole story seemed incredible to him. And he'd been there.

"But if it was that terrific—"

"I wasn't thinking very clearly," Cameron said wearily, running his fingers through his hair. "I wasn't really thinking at all."

"She must have been some broad, all right. Okay, Cameron, we can do this."

"I'm counting on you to write me something that's—restrained and—tasteful."

"Sure thing. But before we begin making this commercial, let's use some logic, here."

Cameron groaned inwardly. Chuck was a brilliant writer, and his absolute favorite reading material was detective novels and some mysteries. He fancied himself an amateur sleuth, and Cameron was sure those instincts were going to come to the fore in about two seconds.

"What about one of those maids in the hotel? I mean, she would have had access, with her key and all. Jeez, Cameron, broads were climbing in the windows when you were interviewing for your 'mother.'"

"Don't remind me."

"We could start by getting a list of employees working that night at the Four Seasons."

It wasn't that bad an idea.

"Take a memo," he said wearily to Mrs. Monahan, who now sat by his desk, steno pad in hand. If she thought this whole situation was too incredible for words, she wisely didn't let a single emotion flit across her face.

"Now," said Chuck, just starting to warm up. "Was there anyone else who might have been at the scene of the—crime. So to speak."

"I appreciate your subtlety."

"Hey, just doing my job. If we can figure out who this dame was, you can save a bundle in production costs."

Cameron paid Chuck by the hour, and he had to concede that if they figured out this woman's identity before he made another info-mercial, it would save Teddy's Toys an astronomical amount of money.

It would save *him* an astronomical amount of money.

"I appreciate your thoughtfulness."

"What about the lawyer?" Chuck accentuated his question by taking the ever-present Cuban cigar out of his mouth and jabbing the air with it for emphasis.

"Mike?" Cameron laughed, the sound mirthless and abrupt. "I don't think so."

"I dunno," Chuck mused. "I saw her out in the front office, and she's quite a looker."

"Mike? Here?" Cameron turned to Mrs. Monahan.

"She had another contract for you to look over, but I referred her to your grandfather."

"Get her in here."

Within minutes, Michaela entered the spacious office.

"You wanted to see me?"

"Did Julian look that contract over?"

"Yes. I was just leaving—"

"Give it to me."

She sat in one of the chairs next to his desk, between Mrs. Monahan and a man she didn't know. He was chewing on the end of a cigar and studying some notes he'd scribbled on the back of an envelope.

"Would you like something to drink?" Cameron offered, scanning the pages of the legal document.

"Coffee would be fine," Michaela replied in a low tone, giving Mrs. Monahan a reassuring smile.

The secretary returned with her cup, then sat back down in her chair by the desk and picked up her steno pad, poised and waiting for whatever Cameron chose to do next.

"Okay," said Chuck. "So it's not one of the maids, and it's not this lady—"

Cameron looked up, a distinctly amused twinkle in his dark blue eyes as he caught Michaela's incredulous expression. "No, I'd say I'm ninety-eight percent sure about that."

"What are you talking about?" Michaela asked him.

Chuck answered her. "The broad that snuck into his bedroom about a month ago and—how can I say this?—rang his chimes, cleaned his clock... ah, you get my drift."

Cameron rolled his eyes as if to say, *Writers*.

"And why couldn't it have been me?"

"What do you mean, Mike?"

"Am I that—staid and dull and boring...?"

"Not at all. But you just don't strike me as the... type."

"Thank you, Mr. Black."

Chuck was watching their entire exchange with quiet fascination. Even Mrs. Monahan had put down her steno pad and was enthralled.

"What's wrong with you today, Mike?"

"Wrong? With me? Oh, nothing at all. Just because you've conveniently consigned me to the roll of a sexless, lifeless fuddy-duddy, I can't see any reason to get upset over something like that."

"Mike, I didn't—"

Teddy Bear Heir   95

"What if I just wanted to unlace my orthopedic shoes, kick up my heels and get crazy one night? What if I lost my head *completely* and wanted to have one night of anonymous, lust-filled, crazed, animal passion? What if I saw the entire experience as a way of feeling *totally* alive for just one night, then resuming my dull, boring, lawyerlike existence?"

"Mike, I didn't mean—"

"Yes, you did. I know exactly what you meant, and I'm not going to let you get away with it! Nope. Just because I wear these businesslike suits and stuffy little blouses, just because I pull on a pair of panty hose every morning and wear sensible heels and quiet, understated jewelry, doesn't mean that the heart of a total, sexual maniac doesn't beat behind this stuffy facade!"

"Mike, I—"

"Coleman, Watts and Burrell happens to be one of the most conservative firms in the city. *And* the most prestigious. But if you hired me and I was on retainer to Teddy's Toys, I might just come into work in tight jeans and a black lace bustier—"

"This I would like to see," Chuck said, leaning back in his chair and chewing on his cigar.

"Or red hotpants and a see-through blouse—"

"I'd buy it," Chuck remarked to no one in particular.

"Or maybe even a minidress and no underwear—"

"Baby, you should be writing this copy," Chuck said, then burst out laughing.

Cameron was staring at Michaela as if he'd never seen her before. But before he could say anything, she gathered up all the papers on his desk, rammed them into her briefcase, then stood and strode out of the room.

"Wow," Chuck said as she reached the door.

"Men!" Michaela said as she threw the office door open. "All of you make me sick!"

The door slammed behind her grand exit and utter silence blanketed the three people that remained in Cameron's spacious office.

"Well," Chuck said after a short pause. "She's either guilty as sin, or that's the most incredible case of PMS I've ever seen."

SHE STRODE to the elevator, her color high, her heart pounding. Who the hell did Cameron Black think he was, to stick her into some preconceived little cubbyhole like that? To judge her as a woman he might like to have sex with, but could never imagine having the sex of his life with?

She jabbed the elevator button with her finger.

Men. They were all pigs. Inconsiderate oafs. Even bedroom skills that would have earned Cameron a place in the Hall of Fame of the Sexual Olympics didn't make up for a basic insensitivity, a gross disregard for her feelings—

She jabbed the elevator button again, and broke a nail. Dropping her briefcase, she kicked the wall.

She'd never in her life lost her temper that way, never in her life done something so foolish. The last thing she wanted to do was call attention to herself, make Cameron believe she might have been in bed with him that night. It was like a scene out of *Crime and Punishment*.

What is wrong with you?

She jabbed the button again, then tore off what was left of her nail. That wasn't like her, either. Normally she would have raced to her manicurist and had it repaired.

Where the hell is that elevator?

"Mike?"

She turned to find Cameron standing in the hallway, staring at her.

"What!"

"I wanted ... to apologize—"

It was the last thing she remembered before she fainted.

JULIAN BLACK started as Mrs. Monahan burst into his office.

"She's fainted! I almost called 9-1-1, but Cameron insisted on taking her to Dr. Mallory—"

"What!"

He was out the door in a shot, racing toward the teaching hospital.

WHEN SHE CAME TO, she was lying in Cameron's arms in the back of a company limousine and he was smoothing her hair out of her eyes.

"Don't talk," he said softly. "Don't move. We'll have you at the doctor's in no time."

"But I'm—"

"Healthy as a horse," he finished for her, putting his finger across her lips to stop her words. "I know. Just humor me, Mike. Let me take care of you."

She closed her eyes.

"I didn't mean to upset you," he said, his voice uncharacteristically rough with emotion. "It's not that I couldn't picture you as a sexual siren, it's just—"

"It doesn't matter—"

"Shh." He smoothed her hair back, and simply held her as the limousine made swift progress through the city streets. Within twenty minutes, she found herself in a doctor's office, with Cameron waiting outside.

"Could you be pregnant?" Dr. Mallory asked conversationally as he took her blood pressure.

"No. That's not an option."

"Why?"

"I...can't."

"When were you actually tested and found to be infertile?"

"Well, I wasn't. I mean, I was married, and we tried for a few years, and he went for tests and it wasn't his problem, so...I knew it was me."

"I see. Then let's consider a pregnancy an option, just in case."

"You're wasting your time. And I'd really rather not be put through a full-scale physical right now."

He patted her arm comfortingly. "I understand. But let's just humor your concerned young man. Let me run some tests, just a few standard procedures. I'll be back from my conference in a few days, and I'll phone you with the lab results."

She hesitated.

"My guess is that you're perfectly all right, and simply overworked. Or stressed."

"Okay. But not too many tests."

He smiled reassuringly. "Just a few. Let's just say I like to cover every possibility."

When she walked out of the examining room and into the waiting room, four pairs of anxious eyes turned toward her.

Cameron, Julian, Mrs. Monahan, and even Chuck.

"I'm fine."

None of them looked convinced.

"Really. I am."

"You're taking the rest of the day off," Cameron announced. "Even if I have to chain you to your bed."

"She's the one," Chuck muttered beneath his breath to no one in particular.

CAMERON DROVE her home, after placing a call to Coleman, Watts and Burrell. Michaela fretted. Two sick days within thirty days, it just wasn't done. Cameron's language shocked her when he told her what he thought of a company that put its so-called principles before the health and welfare of its employees.

He carried her up the steps and inside her house over her protests, and placed her on the overstuffed couch in her living room. Tucking an afghan around her, he proceeded to order in chicken soup from one of the gourmet restaurants the city was so famous for.

Trust Cameron not to simply open a can.

Gomez and Morticia liked him immediately, which Michaela took as a good sign. Or maybe the black-and-white cats liked the smell of the soup. With felines you could never be sure.

"I want you to lie down and try to sleep."

"Cameron, for God's sake—"

"Don't fight me on this one, Mike."

And when she looked up into his eyes, she saw genuine caring there. It wasn't love, but it was the next best thing. The thought that Cameron cared for her made her smile, and she realized how terribly tired she was.

"I am kind of sleepy."

"I know you are. You look exhausted."

She sighed and snuggled beneath the warmth of the crocheted afghan. She had been feeling funny lately, and couldn't seem to shake either the dark circles beneath her eyes or the constant feeling of nausea.

She heard him talking on her phone, and just before she drifted off to sleep, heard him calling Dr. Mallory's office and scheduling a follow-up visit to go over the results of various tests.

THIS TIME, when she went to see Dr. Mallory, only Cameron accompanied her. And luckily, he remained in the waiting room.

"Well," said the doctor as he swept into his office. "I believe congratulations are in order."

"I know. There's nothing basically wrong with me. My father used to always say I was as healthy as a horse."

The doctor's smile widened. "I'll leave you to tell that young man of yours the good news."

"That I'm just fine? He'll be so pleased."

"That you're expecting."

"What?" There was a peculiar roaring sensation in her head and she gripped the sides of the chair she was sitting in. She stared at the older man sitting so calmly behind his desk, and wondered at the fact that one sentence out of his mouth should completely alter her world, tip it on its axis, change her life forever.

"Congratulations, Ms. Larkin. You're going to have a baby."

I'LL LEAVE YOU to tell that young man of yours the good news.

Ha!

She staggered out into the waiting room, and Cameron must have immediately caught on to the fact that something was very wrong.

"Mike?"

She held up her hand, asking him for a moment of silence, and in an effort of total willpower, she composed herself.

Pregnant. Pregnant. You'll be holding a baby in your arms by the end of the year.

You are pregnant with the Teddy Bear heir.

She wondered if Cameron would be happy when she finally had to tell him the news. Maybe Nancy would bear his child, as well, and he could buy them both an island in Tahiti and have his own little tribe of women and children.

Heir and a spare.

Totally inappropriate laughter bubbled out of her as they walked down the hall, took the elevator to the first floor, and got back inside the limousine.

She'd argued with Dr. Mallory furiously, but he'd shown her the test results, and asked after her various symptoms. Now they all made a terrible sort of sense. The dark circles and constant exhaustion. The nausea. The tenderness of her breasts, the crazy, insane behavior, her temper. The smell of food being so much sharper—

A miracle. It was a miracle. She was living proof that miracles still happened in this day and age.

Unless... She wrinkled her nose in thought.

"Mike?"

She jumped. Apparently Cameron had been trying to communicate with her for some time.

"Yes?"

"I have to go back to the office this afternoon, but I'm going to leave the car at your disposal."

She nodded her head, deep in thought. Yes. That would be perfect. She had a little visit to make this afternoon, and a limousine would be the perfect touch.

SHE'D ALWAYS wanted to make a scene in front of her first husband, but had never had the nerve. One of the advantages of being pregnant was that your mind stopped functioning normally, and making a total scene, destroying someone's peace of mind, became an utterly rational, perfectly natural piece of behavior.

This little confrontation had been long overdue.

Ed's law firm wasn't half as prestigious as Coleman, Watts and Burrell, but it was still stuffy enough.

Stuffy enough so that when she went swinging through the door and toward her husband's office, the secretary went into a complete panic.

She must have looked like either an Amazon warrior or an avenging angel, because no one stopped her. Opening the door to Ed's office, she caught him sitting in his desk chair, an attractive woman in her early twenties sitting in his lap and nibbling on his ear.

"You bastard," she hissed.

Ed Buttall jumped out of his leather chair, dumping his current fling onto the rug.

"Michaela!" he squeaked.

"Who is this?" the girl demanded.

"I'm his wife!"

"*Ex*-wife! *Ex!* Danielle, wait a minute, I can explain everything—"

The door slammed shut with a resounding crash, and he turned toward her wearily.

"What the hell do you want?"

"You have a lot of nerve, you worm, making me believe it was all my problem."

"What? What are you talking about?"

"I'm right, aren't I?" He remained quiet. "Aren't I?" she asked again.

He paled beneath his tan, and Michaela knew she had her answer.

"Look, when I went to the doctor—"

"It was you, Ed. It was you all along. And like a *real* man, you let me believe it was all my fault."

"Now, honey—"

"Don't you 'honey' me. You are a bastard, the absolute worst, and the things I'm thinking of doing to you don't even bear repeating—"

The door opened just a crack, and a secretary poked her head in. "Mr. Buttall, your three o'clock is here—"

"They'll have to wait." Michaela calmly crossed the room and smiled at the curious secretary. "Mr. Buttall and I have a very serious matter to discuss."

I COULDN'T BEAR to admit it was me, Michaela. You've got to believe that...

She was out in the garden, weeding. And thinking about that afternoon's encounter with her ex-husband. He'd found out he was sterile early into their marriage and hadn't been able to deal with it at all. Thus he'd maneuvered and manipulated and made her believe it was all her fault.

She closed her eyes as she thought of all the pain she'd endured because of Ed's masculine vanity.

The funny thing was, she'd loved him. Once. And as much as she'd wanted children, she would have stayed with him. No matter what. They could have adopted.

But he'd been sickeningly eager to get rid of her, then he'd married a woman who'd three children of her own. This arrangement, of course, in no way hampered his affairs with his clients.

Ah, Ed, what a man!

Boy, you can pick 'em.

Her father had never liked Ed. He had, however, liked Cameron. And warned her not to get involved with him.

"Unless, my girl, you can get him to give up his heart," Mike Larkin had said. "For without love, there's not much in a man's life, is there?"

Mike Larkin had known what he was talking about. Fiona had been the love of his life, and after she died he had been merely marking time. Oh, there had been a few ladies over the years, the relationships always respectful and discreet. But Mike Larkin had never remarried.

He'd told her once about the night he'd met her mother at a party. "The room faded away, and there was only your mother standing there, so pretty in her party dress. I felt like a big buffoon, but she danced with me, and that was it, my darling. That was it."

Her hands stilled their movement, and she glanced down at the fistful of weeds.

Oh, Pop. You'd be so ashamed of me.

The instant the thought formed, she knew it wasn't true. Mike Larkin would have howled at the moon over the prospect of a grandson or granddaughter, he would have been so happy.

In a funny kind of way, the thought of having a child made her less lonely for her father. It was a continuation of everything her family had been and everything it could be.

She closed her eyes and sat down in the garden with her hand over her abdomen.

Thank you, thank you, oh, thank you.

JOSHUA BURRELL called her into his office that Friday.

"I see you've been taking a lot of sick days," he commented fairly early on in the conversation.

Two days in thirty, and none for the past three years, she thought, struggling to hold on to her temper. Whereas before she could have laughed off the stuffiness and conservative nature of the firm, she now suddenly found it stifling.

"Has everything been taken care of?" he asked, and though his manner was that of a jovial grandfather, she knew what he was asking.

I don't want any messy female emotional details. I just want to know that you will represent this firm in a way that will cause absolutely no complications.

She nodded her head, at the same time knowing that her days with Coleman, Watts and Burrell were numbered.

SHE STARTED to turn one of the bedrooms into a nursery in her spare time. The one luxury she allowed herself was a professional painter, because she simply couldn't stand the smell of the stuff.

The room was painted a soft yellow, and Disney murals graced the walls. Julian, thinking the toys she ordered were for a cousin, gave her a generous discount on anything she wanted from Teddy's Toys.

She didn't go overboard, but her favorite was the golden brown teddy bear that sat in the rocking chair by the window overlooking the back garden. He seemed to be waiting for the little boy or girl that would come play with him, and she liked that feeling.

She wanted to fill her house with love and laughter, to do as good a job raising her son or daughter as Mike Larkin had done with her. Her father had been a terrific single parent, and she could do the same.

And she wondered when, and what, she would tell Cameron.

She didn't have all that much time. According to Dr. Mallory, she was almost eight weeks along, and would begin really showing somewhere in her fourth or fifth month. She already had the bustline of an opera diva, but these days people simply assumed breast enhancement before a pregnancy.

Once she started to show, she would have to take a leave of absence from the firm, as the sight of a pregnant and unmarried woman would not be welcome at such a conservative workplace.

She'd survive. She had enough money in the bank, and could continue paying for her health insurance even if she decided to quit the firm.

She'd be all right.

Her life had a focus now that it hadn't had in months, and as Michaela sat in the nursery, the teddy bear in her lap as she gazed out over the garden, she thought the only thing that could have possibly made her happier was feeling that she had a right to share all of this with Cameron.

But she couldn't. Not just yet. She needed a little more time to come to terms with the fact that she was becoming a mother.

Chapter Six

Nancy turned out to be a fabulous cook.

Cameron realized this fact when he started to gain weight. For Nancy's mother was Southern, and her specialties included buttermilk biscuits, skillet cornbread, coconut cream pie, Southern fried chicken and fried ham with red-eye gravy.

Her pecan pie was to die for.

And she'd passed all her recipes down to her seven daughters, Nancy included.

"Here you go, honey." She placed the plate of fried eggs, ham and grits in front of him. He smiled up at her.

Now why couldn't Nancy have been the one? Blond, nicely bovine, *cute*. Ever so accommodating. Never a bit of trouble. Healthy and uncomplicated.

It's just fate's way of laughing at me.

Nancy didn't even mind that he was involved in finding this mystery woman. She thought it was romantic, and said so at every single opportunity. As she had moved out of her apartment and her room had been promptly rented, he'd told her she could stay at his house as long as she wanted to. After all, he'd already put her through quite a lot of stress, it was the least he could do.

She'd asked him to let her stay for the semester, then she would find another place to live.

Meanwhile his attempts to find his mystery woman were going nowhere, fast.

Chuck's amateur detective work had fizzled out, so the second info-mercial had gone into production a few weeks ago. He'd rushed the job through, auditioning various actors until he'd finally come to the exhausted realization that this was one message he was going to, once again, have to deliver himself.

So Chuck had written the dialogue, and he'd delivered it. Three takes later it was ready for the editing room, and last night it had aired for the first time.

The papers were having a field day.

Teddy Bear Heir Hunts For Mystery Woman! screamed the *Examiner*.

Multimillionaire Cameron Black Loses Girl! said the *Times*.

Search Of The Century! claimed *People* magazine.

Once again, his actions made the foreign papers and Teddy's Toys was deluged with mail. He'd even had a letter from a movie mogul down in Los Angeles who wanted to buy the rights for a miniseries.

Great. Now an entire television audience can see how I've screwed up my love life.

"More coffee?" Nancy stood to his side, coffeepot in hand. He'd told her she didn't have to do all this, that he had servants he paid. But she loved to cook, and he had to admit that what she served up was a whole lot better than his last three cooks had managed.

He took another look at her. A good, long look.

"What are you doing, going to school when you cook like this?"

She blushed prettily, the rose color sweeping up to her hairline. "My cousin said the same thing the other night."

"Well?"

"Well, I— Starting up a restaurant is a huge financial risk."

"Not with food this good."

"I never really thought it was possible."

He came to his decision in a heartbeat. He had excellent business instincts, and had used them to make a bundle of money. If Nancy had even a little help, she couldn't go wrong.

"It is if you find yourself a good business partner. Preferably one with a lot of money."

It took her just a second to realize who he was talking about.

"You mean you'd...?"

He nodded his head.

She threw her arms around him and hugged him. Hard.

The moment was interrupted by a noise in the hall. Cameron frowned as Nancy stepped away from him. He remembered that voice. He remembered that attitude.

The woman burst into the dining room.

He remembered that muumuu.

"I'm sorry, sir, I just couldn't restrain her—" His butler, Browning, looked quietly miserable.

"I told you, me and Cam the Man are old friends—" Sapphire stopped in midsentence. "Do I smell grits?"

Cameron had to laugh. Nancy, the ever-efficient hostess, was already dishing up another plate and setting it in front of the delighted Sapphire.

"It's all right, Browning," Cameron told his relieved servant. The elderly man stepped out of the dining room, but not before giving Sapphire a pointed glare.

Which she didn't even see.

"Girl, these grits are *perfect!* Where's your mama from?"

"Arkansas."

"Humph." There was a short silence while Sapphire tasted everything on her plate. Cameron merely watched her. Trying to contain this woman would be like stopping the tides.

Finally he spoke up.

"Was there a reason you wished to see me?"

"Yes, sir. I saw you on the television last night, and I said to myself, 'Sapphire, what that boy needs is a voodoo charm to help him get that girl back into his life!' So, here I am, and here it is!"

She pulled something out of her purse that looked like a small cloth sack, and set it on the dining room table.

Cameron had excellent people instincts, and knew this woman was totally sincere.

"I just felt sorry for you, Cam. All this money, and you are just a *mess*."

He grinned. "I couldn't have said it better myself."

Another of his talents in business was putting the right teams of people together at the right time.

"Sapphire, do you have any experience in the restaurant business?"

She took a deeply appreciative sip of coffee before answering. "My aunt, she used to run a place in the French Quarter. Made the best red beans and rice for miles around. People would come every Monday to eat her cooking!"

Nancy sat down at the table with another plate, and began to eat her breakfast. Her blue eyes were large and luminous, and Cameron was suddenly quite happy that at least one person out of this entire mess was going to realize her dream.

After business was discussed, Cameron pushed back his chair and was about to leave when Sapphire stopped him.

"I read palms, too."

"You do."

"I'm mighty good."

What the hell. He was game. He gave her his hand and she studied it with fierce concentration.

"You are one proud man."

He smiled.

"But she's gonna get you, this mystery woman."

"I hope so."

"No, no, not just the nasty dance! I mean, she's gonna get your heart. All of it. Body and soul, the best there is. And you're gonna love her for the rest of your life! Look at that love line!" she said, gesturing for Nancy to see his palm.

Cameron felt strangely self-conscious, but squelched the urge to pull his hand from her grasp. Perhaps if he acted as if what she said was of no importance, then it would have no effect.

What was he saying? Of course, it would have no effect.

When the reading was over, Sapphire gave his hand a pat. "You remember what I said. You got a happy life ahead of yourself."

He couldn't help smiling.

As he left, voodoo charm in his briefcase, he heard Sapphire and Nancy planning furiously over a pot of coffee and a basket of sweet potato muffins.

"I've got a catfish recipe that'll make you think you've died and gone to heaven..."

SHE'D KNOWN this day was coming, but had thought she might have just a little more time. Even though Michaela knew her pregnancy barely showed, no one had missed the tremendous expansion of her bustline, or the fact that she spent at least a third of the day in the bathroom.

Dr. Mallory had told her that some unfortunate women seemed to suffer from morning sickness a little longer than the first trimester. And she was one of the unfortunate few.

Still, she'd thought she'd covered her tracks a little better than that.

Today she'd barely made it to Julian's office before slumping down in the chair by his desk, her head in her hands.

She simply felt awful.

She also didn't hear the older man come in. When she finally realized he was in the office with her, she slowly raised her head and gazed into a pair of gentle, twinkling blue eyes.

The eyes of a child, but the soul of a very gentle man.

She swallowed against the tightness in her throat and felt her eyes fill with tired tears.

"How long have you known?" she whispered.

She watched as tears filled his eyes and he came around the desk to the chair next to hers. Taking her hands in his own, he kissed her cheek.

"Thank you," he said. "You have no idea what this child means to me."

"You're not... angry with me?"

"Angry? I'm as happy as Mike Larkin would be if he were here, and the only thing I regret about this moment is that he isn't around so we can go out and raise some hell. It isn't every day a man discovers he's about to become a grandfather. Or a great-grandfather."

His mentioning her father was her undoing, and great sobs worked their way up her chest and out of her mouth. Julian handed her tissues and let her cry herself out, then ordered in some coffee for himself, a glass of juice for her, and sandwiches for both of them.

Mrs. Monahan, tactful as ever, didn't mention the fact that Michaela had obviously been crying.

Once they were alone again, she found she needed the counsel of an older, wiser man. She poured her heart out to Julian, telling him of her fears, her regrets, her reluctance to tell Cameron about the child just yet. And her instinctual knowledge that she was about to be fired from her firm.

"Joshua Burrell has been and always will be a complete ass. Doesn't the man realize that a company is always about its people?"

She sniffed into a tissue.

"You need anything, anything at all, Michaela, you come to me."

"Oh, no! That wasn't why I came here today. There's a contract—"

"It can wait. Now, what time does that slave driver Burrell expect you back?"

"Sometime after lunch."

Julian grinned. "There's a spare office down the hall with a lovely couch in it, just perfect for a nap."

She'd thought she'd cried her fill, but felt tears welling up in her eyes. It seemed she was always exhausted these days, what with both the pregnancy and the burden of her deception.

"That sounds wonderful."

She was almost to the door when she turned and scrutinized Julian.

"How did you know?"

He smiled. "I'd almost lost hope. It was something in your face. A glow. My Mary looked the same way."

She nodded her head, then walked back to the desk, around the side, and gave Julian an awkward hug.

"Thank you," she whispered.

"Ah-hh," he said, hugging her close. "Welcome to the family, little girl."

THE NAP refreshed her, and she washed her face and reapplied her makeup in one of the executive bathrooms. Then she walked back to her office.

Saw the note on her desk.

And knew it was over.

"Michaela, please see me in my office at three."

"OF COURSE you understand the gravity of the situation," Joshua Burrell intoned solemnly.

She'd never disliked him more. She also refused to see things his way.

"I'm not sure that I do."

He cleared his throat, and she knew he was uneasy with her, didn't quite know what to do with her. If she really wanted to disgust him, she'd burst into tears. But she was determined not to give him that particular pleasure.

"You cannot possibly continue to work at a firm as old and established as Coleman, Watts and Burrell while pregnant and unmarried." He paused, just enough to give his next words added emphasis. "That is, unless I misunderstand the situation. Are you married?"

"No."

"Then it should all be quite clear."

She had never been angrier in her life. She loved practicing law, and the thought of this man preventing her from doing just that filled her with a fine, cool rage.

"No, it's not. But I realize that to continue to practice law here would not be in my best interests."

"You've always been bright, Michaela."

"Don't patronize me. You're firing me, and you're going to have a lawsuit on your hands the likes of which you've never seen before."

Joshua Burrell leaned back in his leather chair and smiled. Now he was on familiar ground. It was inconceivable to him that he could lose.

"I don't believe so. You may go."

She left his office, went directly to hers, packed her things, said goodbye to Cassandra, then called a cab and went home.

CAMERON STORMED into his grandfather's office with the intention of simply venting some of his frustration.

Both men had long since disregarded Julian's ultimatum, directly after Cameron had simply told his elderly relative that he wanted to find this woman and not have Nancy feel she was in a marriage in which she would always be second best. Julian had agreed, and except for Cameron's moods, the two men had been getting along remarkably well.

Julian was on the phone.

Teddy Bear Heir   119

"Just wanted you to know, Joshua, that we have always enjoyed working with Michaela Larkin. I consider her extraordinarily talented with contracts and... Oh, I see... Yes, you're making yourself quite clear... No, I don't quite understand..."

Cameron's head went up, his eyes narrowed. Julian's tone had chilled to pure, brilliant ice. He hadn't heard that particular tone of voice in a long time.

"No, I'm sorry. No, we won't be wanting any other lawyer. I shall be getting in touch with her myself..."

Something was terribly wrong.

His grandfather was in a rage, and Cameron listened as the older man delivered his parting shot.

"Frankly, Joshua, I've always considered you a rather sanctimonious bastard." He hung up the phone and turned toward Cameron.

"They fired her."

"Michaela?"

Julian nodded.

"Why?"

"She's in trouble, Cameron."

His grandfather was watching him closely as Cameron reached for the suit jacket he'd carelessly slung over the back of the chair.

"I'm going to her."

Julian nodded his head.

BY THE TIME he reached her office, she was gone.

Cassandra, the petite, blond secretary he'd talked to numerous times, was crying as she packed up her desk.

"They fired you, too?" he asked as he came out of Michaela's empty office.

"I can't stay," she sniffed. "Not after what they did to her. It was so... unfair!"

"Why was she fired?"

She gave him a look that clearly expressed that she thought he knew.

"You can't tell anyone. She didn't want anyone to know, but I knew right away." The delicate blonde dissolved into a new fit of crying.

His heart almost stopped beating at the thought that something might be seriously wrong with Michaela. And it would be just like that bastard, Joshua Burrell, to let her go when she was no longer of any use to his precious firm.

He grasped her upper arms. "What's wrong with her?"

Cassandra eyed him warily.

"On my honor, I won't tell a soul. I just want to do what I can to help her—"

"She's pregnant."

He let go of the young woman, stepped back, steadied himself against her desk.

Pregnant.

Impossible.

The suspicion growing in his mind was too incredible to contemplate. His mind flashed back, remembering.

Chuck, in his office. *Was there anyone else who might have been at the scene of the crime? What about the lawyer?*

Michaela, in his office, in a fine rage. *And why couldn't it have been me?*

Julian, just before he left. *She's in trouble, Cameron.*

Michaela, fainting in the hallway. Looking so very pale. Watching him, her blue eyes wary.

Pregnant.

"How long?" he whispered.

"What?" Cassandra said.

"How far along is she?"

"Almost four months. She wasn't even showing, but she was sick so often that Mr. Burrell started to get suspicious—"

Almost four months... Almost four months ago he'd been in a suite at the Four Seasons.

Almost four months ago he'd been having the most erotic and fulfilling sexual experience of his life.

Could it be...?

Michaela, pregnant with my child.

"Don't get mad at her, okay?"

How like his Mike, to inspire such loyalty.

"Here." He pulled out a business card and scribbled Mrs. Monahan's number on it. "Call tomorrow morning and ask for this woman, she'll see that we find you a comparable job."

The look on her face was all the thanks he needed. Then he was out the door and heading toward Michaela's house.

HE LET himself in the back door, knowing where she kept the spare key.

She wasn't home, and he wondered at that. He would have thought home would be the first place she would head, having just been kicked in the teeth at work. Cameron was sure that Joshua Burrell would have been absolutely ruthless in letting her go.

He thought of her hurting and couldn't bear it.

He thought of her trying to carry this burden all alone, and his heart went out to her.

He went up the stairs and saw the fully decorated nursery, and felt such feelings of rage building inside him that he slammed his fist against the pale yellow wall.

She hadn't just found out. You couldn't put together a nursery like this in a few weeks. There was a lot of love and time and effort that had gone into making this room what it was. What it reflected. Love. And hope.

Why didn't she tell me? he thought with a certain amount of despair. Directly on top of that thought, he wondered, What is she trying to do?

He had never liked feeling out of control, and he didn't like the feelings that swept over him now. He walked over to the rocking chair, set the teddy bear on the floor, and sat down. He watched the early summer sky darken into dusk. His mind had plenty of time to work through the various ramifications of what Michaela had done before he heard her key scrape in the lock downstairs.

He didn't move, just sat in the dark nursery as she came inside and headed straight for the crib. She was carrying a stuffed duck, and she set the toy inside the crib, then turned around and saw him.

She started, frightened for just an instant until she recognized him. Then, even in the dim light, he saw a new fear growing in her eyes and he decided at that exact moment that he was never going to let this woman control his emotions.

Neither of them said a word. They simply stared at each other. Finally, Cameron spoke.

"When were you planning on telling me?"

She knew how damning the entire thing had to look in his eyes. It was obvious, from the way he'd been studying the nursery, that he realized she'd known about her pregnancy for some time.

"No lies, now," he said softly, and she could tell from his tone of voice that he was oh-so-very angry with her.

She nodded her head, not trusting herself to speak. Though she had counted Cameron as one of her closest friends until this moment, she felt as if their relationship was held together by the most tenuous of emotional threads. One wrong move, one false move, and she could sever their connection completely.

She didn't want to do that. The ironic thing was, on the way home from the travel agent and the toy shop, she'd resolved to tell him. Oh, she hadn't expected him to get down on his knees and propose marriage. Cameron Black was a man who lived by his own rules.

But she'd known he would be good to their child, to the result of their tempestuous union. And she'd thought of her father and all he'd meant to her. And she'd realized, deep in her heart, that she wanted this baby to know its father. To be loved and cherished by its father, the way Mike Larkin had loved and cherished her.

She'd been planning to tell Cameron, but she'd been too late. Now she knew how deceptive her actions had to look in his eyes.

"How far along are you?" His voice was deadly calm.

"Almost four months." It amazed her that her voice didn't tremble, that she could form coherent words. She'd thought her heart had broken the night she'd drank Scotch with Cameron in his hotel suite, but now she knew better.

This was heartbreak.

"You were the woman in my hotel room."

"Yes."

"Why?"

She swallowed. He was making this so very difficult for her, and she couldn't really blame him. She had never meant to hurt him this way, but she doubted she'd ever be able to make him see that now.

"I—" She thought of taking the easy way out, of telling him she'd had a little too much to drink and had been a little too lonely. But fierce Irish pride brought her chin up and she faced him head-on.

"I wanted you."

Something in his eyes changed, the most infinitesimal expression. And she knew at that moment that she had a little bit of power in this relationship. If she chose to use it.

"Were you trying to get preg—"

"No."

"You didn't know you could conceive?"

"My husband lied to me. He couldn't have children, but made me believe our childlessness was...my fault."

He nodded his head and was silent for such a long moment that she almost turned and walked out of the nursery.

Then, the most damning question of all.

"Does Julian know?"

She hesitated a fraction too long, and he had his answer.

"He guessed."

She could feel his anger, a shimmering, palpable presence in the sunny little room.

"Was this all some sort of *plan* that the two of you cooked up?"

"*No!*" Her heart was in her mouth as she said the one word, and she wondered how she could ever make him believe her. Trust her. Once she'd wanted him to love her, but that seemed far beyond her grasp.

She gripped the side of the crib to steady herself.

"Did you find this all...amusing?"

She shook her head.

"What were you doing, that afternoon, giving me advice in my office?"

Her shame was absolutely complete. "I—I didn't know I was pregnant then."

"So you would have let me look for you forever."

"I thought... I thought maybe after a while, you'd stop."

"Oh, no. Not when I really want something. You know me better than that."

She couldn't look at him.

"Where were you tonight? After work."

"I was fired."

"I know, I stopped by your office."

She stared at him.

"Cassandra told me."

Neither of them spoke for a moment.

"Where did you go?"

"I went to see my travel agent—"

He got up from the rocking chair with that lithe grace she'd always admired and crossed to her side. Then he slid her purse strap down her arm, took the bag away from her and opened it. The ticket was in his hand in an instant.

"Mexico?"

"I thought... a trip. I've been under a lot of stress."

"Lying does that to you."

Her temper flared. "Haven't you ever been scared?"

"That's what this is about?"

She turned away from him, her frustration complete. Cameron Black, an unemotional machine. Cameron Black, who would never show emotion, never be warm and forgiving like a normal person.

Perhaps she'd been wrong. Perhaps he wasn't at all like Mike Larkin, and didn't have what it took to be a father.

She heard the sound of paper ripping and turned back in time to see the pieces of her ticket being tossed into a Winnie the Pooh wastebasket.

It was too much. She flew at him, began pummeling at his chest with her hands, until he grasped her wrists and hauled her up against him. She was no match for his strength, and knew it.

"You'll have to work out a contract, Mike."

"Get out!"

"I want it all in writing."

"You *bastard!*"

"I'll be generous."

"I don't want anything."

She felt his fingers beneath her chin as he tilted her head up so she had to look at him.

"You still don't understand, do you?"

She looked away.

"Are you all packed?"

She hesitated for a moment, then nodded.

"The cats are taken care of? The house?"

She nodded again. "Where do you think you're taking me?"

"We're going to go somewhere where we won't be interrupted, where no one else will be watching or commenting or coming between us. We're going to straighten out this relationship, Mike, and come away with some sort of contract."

He had one of her wrists in his, and now practically dragged her toward the door of the nursery.

"No! I won't go—" He interrupted her by sweeping her up into his arms and carrying her down the stairs and out the door, taking her keys out of her purse and locking up the house while she struggled in his arms.

Once inside the car, he asked his driver to take them to the airport.

"You can't do this—"

He merely looked at her.

She knew how she had to appear, after struggling with him down the stairs and into the car. Now she desperately sought to calm her racing heart, to try to appear in control of the situation.

This was the twentieth century, wasn't it? He couldn't just sweep into her life and kidnap her, even if she was carrying his child.

She tried the door. Locked.

He smiled.

She tapped on the glass separating them from the driver.

No response.

They were headed for San Francisco airport, and from there, she didn't know where. She was going to be alone with a man who practically despised her.

What would he do to her?

Michaela decided to try one last time.

"Cameron," she began, trying to keep her voice steady. "I don't want this to happen. I don't want any sort of contract between us. I don't want anything from you." She could feel her face flushing bright red. "I don't want to be a kept woman."

DOUBLE YOUR ACTION PLAY...

"ROLL A DOUBLE!"

Peel off label place inside

**CLAIM 4 BOOKS
PLUS A FREE
GIFT**

ABSOLUTELY FREE!

SEE INSIDE..

NO RISK, NO OBLIGATION TO BUY...NOW OR EVER!

GUARANTEED

PLAY "ROLL A DOUBLE" AND GET FIVE FREE GIFTS!

HERE'S HOW TO PLAY:

1. Peel off label from front cover. Place it in space provided at right. With a coin, carefully scratch off the silver dice. Then check the claim chart to see what we have for you – FREE BOOKS and a gift – ALL YOURS! ALL FREE!

2. Send back this card and you'll receive brand-new Harlequin American Romance® novels. These books have a cover price of $3.50 each, but they are yours to keep absolutely free.

3. There's no catch. You're under no obligation to buy anything. We charge nothing – ZERO – for your first shipment. And you don't have to make any minimum number of purchases – not even one!

4. The fact is thousands of readers enjoy receiving books by mail from the Harlequin Reader Service® months before they're available in stores. They like the convenience of home delivery and they love our discount prices!

5. We hope that after receiving your free books you'll want to remain a subscriber. But the choice is yours – to continue or cancel, anytime at all! So why not take us up on our invitation, with no risk of any kind. You'll be glad you did!

©1990 Harlequin Enterprises Limited

NOT ACTUAL SIZE

You'll look like a million dollars when you wear this lovely necklace! Its cobra-link chain is a generous 18" long, and the multi-faceted Austrian crystal sparkles like a diamond!

"ROLL A DOUBLE!"

PLACE LABEL HERE

SCRATCH HERE

SEE CLAIM CHART BELOW

154 CIH ANEP
(U-H-AR-04/94)

YES! I have placed my label from the front cover into the space provided above and scratched off the silver dice. Please rush me the free books and gift that I am entitled to. I understand that I am under no obligation to purchase any books, as explained on the back and on the opposite page.

NAME _____

ADDRESS _____ APT. _____

CITY _____ STATE _____ ZIP CODE _____

DETACH AND MAIL CARD TODAY!

CLAIM CHART

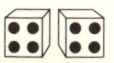

⚄ ⚄	4 FREE BOOKS PLUS FREE CRYSTAL PENDANT NECKLACE
⚅ ⚂	3 FREE BOOKS
⚅ ⚅	2 FREE BOOKS

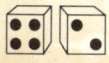

CLAIM NO. 37-829

Offer limited to one per household and not valid to current Harlequin American Romance® subscribers. All orders subject to approval.
©1990 Harlequin Enterprises Limited
PRINTED IN U.S.A.

THE HARLEQUIN READER SERVICE®: HERE'S HOW IT WORKS

Accepting free books puts you under no obligation to buy anything. You may keep the books and gift and return the shipping statement marked "cancel". If you do not cancel, about a month later we will send you 4 additional novels, and bill you just $2.89 each plus 25¢ delivery and applicable sales tax, if any.* That's the complete price, and – compared to cover prices of $3.50 each – quite a bargain! You may cancel at any time, but if you choose to continue, every month we'll send you 4 more books, which you may either purchase at the discount price...or return at our expense and cancel your subscription.

*Terms and prices subject to change without notice. Sales tax applicable in N.Y.

BUSINESS REPLY MAIL
FIRST CLASS MAIL   PERMIT NO. 717   BUFFALO, NY

POSTAGE WILL BE PAID BY ADDRESSEE

HARLEQUIN READER SERVICE
3010 WALDEN AVE
PO BOX 1867
BUFFALO NY 14240-9952

NO POSTAGE
NECESSARY
IF MAILED
IN THE
UNITED STATES

If offer card is missing, write to : The Harlequin Reader Service, 3010 Walden Ave., P.O. Box 1867, Buffalo, NY 14269-1867

He didn't touch her physically, but his gaze raked over her. First she felt a chill up her spine, then she was suffused with heat.

"You still don't get it, do you?" he said, his voice low and rough. Just for her. "I'm through asking."

Chapter Seven

It was a beautiful evening for flying.

They reached the airport with no trouble, traffic was light. Once out on the airstrip, Michaela realized they were going to be using the company jet.

She'd flown on it once before, when Julian had loaded it up with toys and gone to the scene of a disastrous flood. One of the principles of Teddy's Toys was to give back, especially to children. Julian considered them to be the innocent victims of so much unhappiness, and he gave away a considerable amount of his company's product every year, especially at Christmas.

Now, as she and Cameron boarded the luxurious jet, she had no idea where he was taking her. Oddly, there was a certain amount of relief in letting him take charge.

Ever since she discovered she was pregnant, she'd thought of what he would do when she told him. In her wildest, most romantic dreams, he'd looked deeply into her eyes, declared his love for her, and been so happy about the life they had created together.

That was definitely a dream. In reality, she wasn't really sure how he felt about the baby.

Since they'd boarded the plane, they hadn't spoken. He still hadn't told her where the plane was taking them. When she'd asked, all he did was escort her to a seat. He made sure she had a pillow, blanket and a drink, then left her to her own devices.

On a plane this size, it would be difficult for the two of them to avoid each other for too long. But with Cameron, she wouldn't be surprised.

As she had no fear of flying, she simply looked out the window, watching the lights of the city grow fainter and fainter. Then they were up among the clouds.

Michaela didn't know where she was going, she only knew she was headed toward her destiny with Cameron.

THE ONE flight attendant shook her shoulder gently, and Michaela came out of a deep sleep.

"I'm sorry to disturb you," he whispered. "But this phone call seemed urgent."

She took the phone out of his hand, already knowing who it had to be.

"Julian?"

"Michaela. How are you?"

More and more, the elderly man seemed to be filling part of the void left by her father's recent death.

"Not so good."

"He was angry."

"Mmm...that about covers it."

"He gets that way. Black Irish moods. He's that way with me."

"That's a relief. I thought he saved it all up for me."

Julian laughed. "They phoned me from the airport. They always do when the corporate jet is being used. It didn't take me too long to figure out Cameron was probably taking you away."

She swallowed against the tightness in her throat. "I don't think it's going to be much of a vacation."

"Oh, no, my dear girl. It's quite a necessary step. Do you like fairy tales?"

For a moment she thought Julian was starting to go senile. Fairy tales? At a time like this?

"You mean, like Bluebeard, where she finds out he's really a monster and he tries to kill her?"

Julian chuckled. "I hope my great-grandchild has some of your spirit."

She couldn't help smiling.

"If you study your fairy tales, you know there's always a moment where he takes her to his kingdom, a place where he alone rules and his word is law."

"I thought that was the office," she said dryly.

Julian laughed. "Oh, my dear, no. I may appear to be an old fuddy-duddy, but I still consider myself the acting head of Teddy's Toys."

"Of course," she murmured, ashamed of herself.

"Don't worry. I know you meant no harm. No, my grandson is taking you to his island—"

"Where?"

"Second star to the right and straight on till morning."

"Julian!"

"It's in the Caribbean. Somewhere near Aruba. It's quite well hidden, actually, and that was one of the reasons he bought it."

"Is it... totally isolated?"

"The house is, and I'm sure that's where he'll take you. There's a tiny village down by the shore, but I don't know how much you'll see of it."

She was silent for a long moment.

"His bark is much worse than his bite, my dear."

"He thinks I deliberately tricked him."

"He'll understand it all, in time."

Now she knew who Julian reminded her of. As well as Kris Kringle, the elderly man reminded her of Merlin, King Arthur's wizard.

"You know him better than I do," she finally admitted.

"You know him in a way no one else ever will," Julian replied softly. "He's angry with you, Michaela, for you've gotten closer to him than anyone else. It frightens him."

"Why?" she whispered, hoping he would give her an answer that made sense.

"You know how his parents died?"

"Yes."

"He was five at the time." Julian took a deep breath. "It took him almost a year after their deaths before he would speak."

She couldn't answer him as the enormity of that statement sunk into her consciousness.

"Mary and I did our best, but I believe there was a part of him we were never truly able to reach. He's afraid of deep feeling, Michaela, and I'm sure his feelings for you are quite powerful."

"That was—" She forced herself past her embarrassment. "That's just sex."

"No. That's magic. Your father was wise enough to hold on to it when he found it, wasn't he?"

"Yes," she whispered.

"And I knew the minute I saw my Mary."

Tears welled in her eyes. "Oh, Julian, I've made such a total mess of things."

"No, no, you haven't. You see, the men in my family are a funny bunch. They love only once, but when they do, it's for this lifetime and beyond."

"What do you mean?"

"I know I'm going to see my Mary again. I'm sure of it. There was no one else for me, and there's no one else for Cameron but you. And this baby."

"Julian." She was so deeply ashamed, but she had to confide in someone. "He wants a contract."

Julian laughed softly. "Of course. The stubborn boy is right on schedule. If he has a contract, he thinks he can control things."

"Should I let him have one drawn up?"

"Let him do whatever he wants. He's already lost, and it's a feeling he's never liked, not since he was a little boy."

"Then why is he taking me away. Control?"

"Exactly."

"Do you think the idea of a baby frightens him?"

"No. *You* frighten him."

She considered this for a long moment, comforted by knowing Julian was on the other end of the line.

"So he's trying to win."

"Exactly. If you think of love as a game, my girl, you've already won."

"I don't want to think of it that way."

"Good. For if you think of it as love, both of you win. For the rest of your lives."

"He's told me he doesn't believe in love."

"Words, my darling girl. Words. He loves you. I saw it in his eyes. At the office. I'll have you know, you're the reason I came up with that foolish ultimatum in the first place."

"Truly?"

"Truly." Julian lowered his voice. "Oh, I was selfish enough to want a great-grandchild, but above all else I wanted to see my grandson happy. I know it's not wise to meddle in your children's affairs, but I couldn't help myself."

She smiled. "Thank you."

"And do you love him?"

"Oh, Julian, from the first moment I saw him."

"I knew it. Well, I'm going to let you get back to sleep. Now, take your vitamins, drink plenty of milk, and don't let that grandson of mine snarl at you too much."

"Julian?"

"Yes?"

"I love you."

SHE WOKE to the sound of the sea, and stepped out onto the balcony connected to her bedroom.

Though she considered herself spoiled, living in a city like San Francisco with its incredible weather, restaurants, and culture, there was something to be said for an island in the Caribbean. The sea stretched far out to the horizon, and the house, up on a hill, commanded a magnificent view of the sparkling water.

She smiled. Rich people were so strange. They used simple words like "house" and "car" to describe things like mansions and limousines. This "house," as Julian had referred to it over the phone, was nothing short of a palace.

The garden was terraced, and stretched down the hillside. Michaela caught a glimmer of blue, farther down, and assumed it was the pool.

She went back inside and explored her room, discovering that someone had carefully unpacked her bags. They'd arrived late at night, she'd been asleep and not much more alert once she'd been awakened. Truthfully, she didn't remember much of her journey to this house, and now she realized that if someone had unpacked her clothing, then Cameron had to have some sort of a staff.

It was tempting to contemplate behavior that would have suited a Gothic heroine. She could swiftly dress, race down the stairs and demand to be taken off the island as soon as possible. She could convince them that their boss was a madman, terrorizing others with his various whims—

But she wasn't a Gothic heroine. And she wasn't terrified. And whatever was to go down between her and Cameron had to be figured out, for her child's sake if for no other reason. So she would act like the mature woman that she was, even if her insides sometimes felt like total mush.

She showered, then looked through her clothes. She'd packed some maternity outfits, as she'd been originally planning to schlepp around in the stuff at home. It had promised to be exhausting, holding in her stomach all the time at Coleman, Watts and Burrell, and she'd wanted to get comfortable in the privacy of her house.

But most of the maternity outfits that were commercially available had repulsed her. Polka dots, flower prints, cutesy plaids and designs she wouldn't have wanted to have seen on a couch let alone a pregnant female. Who were the manufacturers of America trying to kid? She'd had sex. That much was obvious. It didn't make sense, trying to make herself look childish again.

So she'd ordered some extremely sophisticated maternity clothes from the European catalogs, and now pulled out a pair of white shorts and a top with graceful, billowing sleeves. She dressed quickly, applied sunscreen, made sure she had her prenatal vitamins in her bag, and decided to try to find out where the food was served.

Cameron was sitting out on the back patio at a charming breakfast table, reading the paper. Her heart sped up when she spotted him, then revved up a little more when she discovered he was wearing only a pair of faded cutoffs. He didn't look up as she sat down, and she took that as a good sign.

Maybe they could get through this supposed holiday, after all.

A competent-looking woman, her gray hair pulled back in a bun, approached the table and asked her what she wanted for breakfast.

"Just some toast. And juice."

"And some eggs," Cameron muttered, never taking his eyes off the front page of the *Wall Street Journal*.

And a good morning to you, Mr. Control.

She bit her lip to keep her temper in check, and reconsidered telling Cameron to give it a rest. Julian was right, she had to look at this whole thing from a totally different perspective if she had any hope of remaining emotionally intact.

"Eggs would be fine."

That got his attention. He glanced up from the paper and studied her, his eyes coolly assessing. Apparently he wasn't used to her agreeing with him.

She smiled at him, and wished she'd thought to bring a book to breakfast. Or a mini TV. She would, tomorrow.

He set the newspaper down, and she willed her stomach to stop its wild flip-flopping. This wasn't morning sickness. This was Gothic heroine terror.

"What would you like to do today?" he asked.

She hadn't expected that from him. She'd thought he would drag her into his den after breakfast and they would immediately start pounding out the finer details of the contract.

He'd caught her off guard, and she didn't like it. She didn't want him to be charming or—God forbid—understanding. She wanted him to be surly, to come out of the ring snarling, to be such an utter boor that her mind wouldn't drift back to that incredible evening at the Four Seasons—

Sex.

Her brain shifted into high gear. Sex. Of course, that was it. They were alone in this huge mansion— excuse me, in the "house"—and unless he had plans for a few other guests showing up, she was the only female entertainment for miles around.

Sex. What a stumbling block.

She smiled at him sweetly and was gratified to see that he looked a bit nervous.

"What would *you* like to do today?" she asked.

He knew what she was up to. She could tell by the slight grin that barely formed on his handsome mouth.

"Oh, I'll leave it up to you."

Great. Alphonse and Gaston, trapped on an island.

"Well," she said cheerfully as a plate of soft-boiled eggs and toast was set down in front of her, "I thought I might catch some rays out by the pool."

He nodded his head.

"Maybe swim a little—"

He agreed.

"Then perhaps take in a movie tonight."

He frowned.

Aha! He does want to keep me a prisoner!

"I don't believe there's a movie theater on the island."

"Oh."

"But I did install a private screening room, and several friends of mine have been generous enough to give me rough cuts of their upcoming movies."

The rich are different from you and me.

"That would be swell."

So, it's humor her today, is it Cameron? Well, I'm just going to wait it out. Be as charming as you want, I'm not letting my guard down until you move in for the kill. I'm going to be ready for you. I'm going to—

"You've got some egg on your blouse."

She glanced down to where he was staring and noticed that her bustline—now more of a massive shelf than an actual part of her body—had caught a piece of egg she'd spilled. She dabbed at it with a napkin.

"Thanks."

I can't stand this! We've slept together, talked together, argued contract law together, made a baby together, and we can't even talk like two normal human beings! I can't endure day after day after day of this—

Wait! It's exactly what he wants. He wants you to get all upset and lose your cool and then you'll be at his mercy, exactly where Mr. Control wants you—

Heh-heh. Not a chance, bud.

She smiled sweetly at him, and it felt as if her lips were going to calcify and fall off. He studied her for the briefest of seconds, and her intuition told her he didn't have the slightest idea what she was up to.

Excellent.

She finished her breakfast and pushed her chair back.

"How about meeting me down by the pool in, say, forty-five minutes?"

He didn't look up from his paper. "Fine."

PREGNANCY, to her way of thinking, had not exactly improved her body.

She'd never been one of those women who had yearned for enormous breasts. She'd been quite content with what had been doled out genetically. Now, though the function of those same breasts didn't bother her, she did wish there were times when they were a little less obvious.

She loved to sleep on her stomach. That was getting harder and harder.

She liked looking sleek and pantherish in her black maillot, lying by the pool like a dangerous big cat waiting for her prey.

Now, struggling with perhaps the one solid-colored maternity swimsuit she'd been able to find in North America, she realized that her and Cameron's little tête-à-tête by the pool was going to resemble the opening act at Sea World.

"He's driving me insane," she muttered as she struggled with the straps. "No one is that calm and controlled all the time. Unless they're dead."

Her mind flashed back to that one evening when Cameron hadn't been in control at all. Not at all.

She ran a brush through her hair, flung it down on the bed, and eyed herself in the full-length mirror that someone had so thoughtfully put in the large bedroom. One thing that could be said for only eyeing yourself in the medicine cabinet mirror was that you could delude yourself into thinking that at least your face didn't look fat.

This sunning by the pool was not a good idea.

Mr. Bronze God looked good in anything, and a bathing suit would show off his obvious masculine charms. While she, instead of looking like a fertility goddess, looked more like Willy of *Free Willy* fame.

And she was only four months along.

Breathe, breathe. Calm, calm. Think calming thoughts.

She calmed down, just slightly, and headed toward the pool.

HE WASN'T there yet, so she threw her towel on one of the chairs and headed toward deep water. She paddled around for a while, and the sensation of being off her feet was fabulous.

Ah, you're not that huge. Not yet, anyway. And what does he expect, for God's sake? You're pregnant!

The pool was located on one of the terraces that got the most sunshine, and she enjoyed it, floating in the water, letting the tension seep out of her body, feeling relaxed for the first time in a long time...

Then she opened her eyes and saw him.

His swimsuit couldn't have been any smaller if he'd simply taken a can of black spray paint and applied it to himself. Normally she didn't like such brief swimsuits on men, but on Cameron, the effect was—

Devastating.

Part of what made it so sexual was that he was totally unselfconscious of his near nakedness. Part of what made it so incredible was that she hadn't had a chance to look at him that night in the hotel room.

Now she could look all she wanted, and as much as she hated to admit it, she liked what she saw.

It wasn't fair, that one man should have such a criminal advantage in the battle of the sexes. There wasn't an ounce of fat on that body, and muscles rippled in all the right places. He even had the perfect amount of body hair.

She did a surface dive and sank into the water.

She felt the water shift as he dove in.

She moved away from him, thinking she would have preferred sharing the swimming pool with the shark from *Jaws*.

You're in control here, you're in control, you're in control...

He touched her arm and she surfaced with a yelp.

"What!"

He backed off, and she saw genuine concern in his eyes.

"You looked like... you were struggling."

She pushed wet hair out of her eyes and, as unobtrusively as possible, put a little distance between them.

"No, that's just the way I swim."

"Oh. I'm sorry."

"It's okay."

She was dying to scream at him, almost trembling with the need to demand a less superficial interaction between them, but she wasn't going to be the first one to break. If he could be sophisticated, so could she. If he could look on this as a cross between a vacation and a business trip, so could she.

But she didn't want to.

A business trip, a deal negotiated to define three lives that should have been bound together by love?

Her eyes stung, and she dived back into the water before he could notice.

HE NOTICED.

And he thought of her as one of the bravest women he knew. She had spirit, she had courage, and he was increasingly afraid that she had his heart.

He'd been so angry that she'd kept her pregnancy a secret for so long. To his way of thinking, she should have called him the minute she found out. That lack of trust had, in his mind, done a lot of damage to the friendship they'd built up over the months they'd worked together.

Now he wasn't sure what he wanted.

He knew, deep in his heart, that he didn't need any sort of contract with Michaela. The words he'd said had been meant to hurt, had been meant to take away the sting of his own rage. But the funny thing was, they hadn't. He'd seen the hurt he'd inflicted, and only felt worse.

In some ways he regretted the impulse that had led him to practically kidnap her and force her to come to his house in the Caribbean. In retrospect, it seemed a childish, almost too macho thing to do.

But maybe he could still salvage things. God knows they'd both needed time away from their jobs, and Michaela's firing had provided that opportunity. They were, by nature, workaholics, and it seemed as if this baby had been thrown into the works of their lives partly as life's way of getting them both to look at the way they were living.

To get them to slow down. Enjoy each other. Take some time for the all too human elements of existence.

Work couldn't sustain a person indefinitely, but it was so damn seductive. Work was safe. Work was a controlled area of his life. Work gave him a certain release, it was so predictable and pleasurable.

Michaela would be astonished if she knew how out of control he felt around her.

Though she hadn't come out of the pool yet, he'd already visually assessed her body and found it beautiful. Memories of that first night they'd spent together had haunted him, for once he'd known the woman in his arms hadn't been Nancy, he'd tried to remember her by touch.

Her body had been delicate, but strong. Her breasts were neither small nor large, but exquisitely sensitive, and the skin so smooth and hot. Her stomach had been flat, but the muscles had quivered as he'd kissed his way down her body...

Now that same body looked riper and fuller and so much more desirable. It took exquisite control on his part to ensure she didn't know how much he wanted her.

He walked up the cement steps, out of the shallow end of the pool, then lay down on one of the chaise longues, with his face in his arms. The sun felt warm on his back, but he kept his face hidden, sensing that Michaela might need some privacy to come out of the pool.

He guessed right. She waited about ten minutes and must have just assumed he'd fallen asleep. He heard her step out of the pool, tentatively, like a deer entering a strange clearing in the woods. Then he heard her lie down on one of the lounge chairs across from him.

He lay very still, wondering what to do, and when he finally raised his head and glanced at her, the sight brought a smile to his lips.

She was fast asleep, her face against one of the outdoor pillows. Stretched out on the chaise longue, in full sunlight, there was a good chance she'd sunburn. Not wanting that to happen, and wanting to touch her so very badly, Cameron slowly sat up, then stood and walked over to her lounge chair.

Asleep, she looked so much more vulnerable. And he wondered what might have happened if she'd simply stayed in his hotel bedroom, spent the night. Let him draw back the heavy drapes in the morning, flood the room with light, and see her face.

There was an outdoor mattress in the shade of several palm trees on the far side of the pool. Gently, so as not to awaken her, Cameron lifted Michaela in his arms and carried her to the mattress. He lowered her gently so she remained asleep the entire time.

He covered her with a large towel, then stood looking down at her.

And he knew that, had he found her that morning at the Four Seasons, he would have never let her out of his life. Had she not been able to have children, he wouldn't have given a damn. Had Teddy's Toys gone to the Foundation for Play, he wouldn't have cared.

He'd loved her from the beginning.

He could even remember the first day he'd seen her. She'd been rushing into the main office, hair flying, eyes sparkling, a determined look on her face. She'd been on her way into Julian's office with a contract, and he'd wondered who she was.

Julian had called him in, and he'd been fascinated by how she had taken the finer points of the contract apart, by the skill and poise and immense amount of knowledge of the law she'd possessed.

He'd been even more fascinated by the way she looked, and by the thoughts he'd had about getting her into his bed. He'd known there was a certain chemistry between them, but nothing had prepared him for that one glorious night.

Now, looking back, he was sure Julian had seen that attraction. That mutual fascination. The old man had known. It had probably been the impetus behind the entire ultimatum.

Until Michaela's infertility had thrown a wrench into the works.

Until she'd had the courage to confront, head-on, what neither of them had had the courage to face until that night four months ago.

I wanted you, she had said.

I wanted you.

He was down on his knees on the mattress before he even knew what he was contemplating. He was lifting the towel and sliding beneath it, moving toward her, fitting his body against hers. And not even trying to control the start of an arousal that was painful in its intensity.

She turned in her sleep and snuggled against him, trusting and secure. Her head fit against his shoulder, and he liked the way she felt against him, so soft and warm and smooth.

I wanted you.

He shifted slightly and kissed her on her forehead.

"I want you, too," he whispered. "And I'm going to have you."

Then he settled back, their bodies touching their entire length, and waited for her to wake from her dream.

SHE AWOKE to the realization that she was plastered against him, snuggled up in the most intimate fashion, and anyone coming upon the two of them would have thought they'd been lovers for months instead of just that one night.

Raising her head slowly, she saw that he was looking down at her. She'd been lying with her head on his shoulder, and now their faces were barely inches apart.

"Good nap?" he asked softly.

She nodded her head.

Michaela wondered what they were going to do. Obviously they couldn't live together on this island for long without their strange mutual attraction getting them in some kind of trouble. But she wanted more than a modern-day relationship. It was kind of like the house-and-car thing. The words didn't reflect what was really going on, what the reality of the situation was.

She didn't revere the institution of marriage. You couldn't work with the law and not realize that marriage had taken quite a beating in the last few decades. No, what she wanted was love, and the more time that went by, the more she was beginning to believe that maybe Cameron really didn't have that particular emotion inside him to give.

Loyalty, friendship, protection—those were qualities he could muster. But love—she wasn't sure anymore.

It was so wonderfully comforting, lying against him, feeling the heat of his body and smelling that warm, masculine scent that was his alone. But she had to get up, had to get away from him, before things got out of hand.

Reluctantly she sat up, moved away from him, and pushed her hair out of her eyes.

"Mike, we need to talk," he said.

She nodded her head again. Words seemed to have deserted her. Usually she was articulate and competent, wordy, with a lawyer's flair for words. Now, at a time when she so desperately needed to tell Cameron how she truly felt, she couldn't seem to summon the necessary thoughts into her head.

"I want to marry you," he said.

I want to marry you. Not I love you. I can't live without you. I need you to make my life complete.

I want to marry you.

She held in the sigh that threatened to escape, sensing he wouldn't be too flattered by that particular response. Then she realized that she'd waited too long with her answer, and that was answer enough.

But what about the child she carried? Didn't he or she deserve parents who were married? Who were ready to face the responsibilities of bringing a young life into the world as a united couple? Shouldn't she merely sacrifice her own wants and needs to the needs of her child?

And shouldn't a child know that he or she has parents who truly love each other?

That moment decided her with a brilliant, crystal clarity. For, as she had grown up, Mike Larkin had told her literally hundreds of stories about her mother, and the one thing she had been absolutely certain of, the one thing that had become the bedrock of her entire emotional existence, was that her parents had always loved each other.

She couldn't give her child any less.

"I can't," she whispered.

The silence was deafening, but she noticed that he didn't move away from her.

"Any particular reason?" he asked, and she could sense the anger and hurt pride beneath the surface of his civilized words.

"I need love, Cameron."

That silenced him.

She had to do something to fill the silence. She felt so miserable about the way things were turning out. For one moment she wished she'd never given in to the temptation to satisfy her curiosity, never walked into that master bedroom, never lain down on that bed, and never been the aggressor in starting that particular night of lovemaking that had so profoundly changed both their lives.

And created another.

"I want this child to know that his or her parents truly love each other. I want to give my baby what my father gave me. I couldn't live in a house with you and pretend. It would kill something inside of me to love you and know you didn't love me in return."

She'd said it. Albeit in a roundabout way. But she'd admitted she loved him. Surely he'd known already. A man didn't get to his position, negotiate shrewd deals and run a multimillion-dollar company without an ability to read people. And Michaela knew that when she looked at him, much as she wanted to hide it, her love for him was right there in her eyes.

She knew he'd heard her, but he said nothing in return. Instead, he slowly took hold of both her upper arms and pulled her toward him on the outdoor mattress. They were both on their knees, and now, feeling his touch, Michaela could sense herself weakening.

"I care for you more than I've ever cared for any other woman," he said roughly, and she could see genuine pain in his dark blue eyes.

She closed her own and willed herself to be strong. She knew Cameron. How difficult it was for him to admit even that.

How easy it would be to simply give in and let him take care of her and the baby. How easy it would be to overlook something that was as necessary to her soul as the dappled sunlight and the warm rain to the tropical ferns surrounding the pool area.

She couldn't speak, the pain was so great. She merely shook her head.

"I'll claim the child as mine."

Her head came up, and sudden understanding dawned.

"Oh, Cameron, I'd never stop you from seeing your child! I don't plan on leaving San Francisco, and I'd never prevent you from being a good father. And I know you will be. I just can't contemplate a relationship without love."

"I don't think I can give you that, Mike."

Oh, it was so hard. She'd known this moment had to come, known from the moment she'd seen him in the baby's nursery, so angry. She'd known they would have to confront what their relationship—God, she hated that word!—was going to be. She'd known all of this, but nothing in the way of knowing had prepared her for the enormity of the emotional pain.

It was beyond crying, beyond any sort of physical display of emotion. It was something that touched her soul, and froze it. And at that moment Michaela felt dead, for she knew, with every instinct she possessed, that Cameron was the only man she would ever love.

Maybe one miracle is all you get in this lifetime.

The child they'd created together was surely a miracle. She had never expected to be a mother, and now, by Christmas, she would hold her baby in her arms. Maybe it was the same for her as for her father. The love of a child, but no love from a spouse.

She felt her chin come up, felt that familiar surge of courage and sheer, raw will. She could get through this. She would survive. She would simply do what she had to do.

"I'm sorry, Cameron."

He looked away, and she knew he was in pain, as well. And a part of her wished she were a more compliant, less exacting woman. She knew women who entered these sorts of arrangements every single day. Compliance in exchange for financial and physical protection. She'd wondered at it at first, then simply accepted it. Maybe by the time they reached that moment of acceptance, they were simply too beaten down by the world to even care anymore.

She couldn't do the same. She had no excuse. She had her health, an excellent income, and all her skills as a lawyer. She would be independent, if very lonely, and she would throw her emotional energies into raising her child.

A fulfilling life, if a lonely one.

She took a deep breath. "I'd like to go home."

He was looking at her as if he'd never truly seen her before. Then he slowly nodded his head, stood, and walked away from the pool.

SHE CRIED later that night, in the shower. Then she packed all her belongings and lay down on the large bed in her room, suddenly exhausted. A little nap before dinner wouldn't hurt.

The next thing she knew, Cameron was gently shaking her awake. She looked up into his eyes and saw total, naked fear.

Something was very wrong.

She reached for his hand, grasped it, squeezed his fingers tightly. And in that gesture, she gave him everything, her support, her love, her courage and her soul.

"Tell me," she whispered.

"It's Julian. He's in the hospital."

Chapter Eight

They flew home that same evening.

There was a lot more to this emergency than Julian's sudden hospitalization. As both Cameron and Michaela listened to Mrs. Monahan over the jet's speaker phone, the reason for the intense stress in Julian's life became quite clear.

"He didn't want to worry you," she said, her voice hoarse and nasal. She was calling from the hospital, and had already given them an update of Julian's condition, which was stable if not good. "He knew the two of you were trying to work things out, and he wanted that more than anything."

"We have worked things out," Michaela said calmly, and Cameron once again looked at her as if he'd never seen her before. Cool, calm, professional—and beautiful.

Julian had been plagued by a lawsuit. A woman claimed that she had thought up the bear that had become the Teddy's Toys' logo. That bear, Bandit Bear, was a cuddly brown bear with a masklike marking on his face. His image was on every single toy and game produced by Teddy's Toys.

"Coleman, Watts and Burrell has taken on the case," Mrs. Monahan said, and Cameron could sense Michaela tensing beside him.

Joshua Burrell had never liked Julian, and Cameron was sure their last exchange over the phone hadn't endeared the older man to the lawyer. Taking on this woman's lawsuit seemed almost a deliberate act of malice.

"But Bandit Bear was thought up almost fifty years ago," Michaela replied in answer to something that Mrs. Monahan said. Cameron brought his thoughts back to the present with a vengeance.

"This woman says she thought him up first, and has some sort of submission to back up her claim. She insists that, when she was a little girl, she drew a picture of Bandit for some sort of contest. She didn't win, and then, according to her story, a remarkably similar bear became the company's logo."

"That damn contest," Cameron muttered. "Burrell is going to make this a personal vendetta. He's going to ensure Julian is utterly humiliated."

"Cameron," Mrs. Monahan said soothingly over the speaker phone. "I've tried, over the last five years, to make Julian see he can no longer be the acting head of the company. He should've given it over to you years ago."

Cameron closed his eyes against the sudden sting of moisture. Julian was a law unto himself. He hadn't given up the company because he'd wanted to see him happily settled down with a wife and children. He was certain of this.

They'd already learned that Julian had simply collapsed in his office after one particularly unpleasant call from Joshua Burrell. Mrs. Monahan had found him on the floor, gasping for breath, and had called an ambulance. Once at the hospital, it had been determined that Julian Black hadn't had a heart attack, but had simply fallen prey to exhaustion and stress.

At his age, it was a dangerous combination.

"We'll be coming directly to the hospital," Cameron told the secretary.

"I'll have the car waiting."

"JULIAN," Michaela said softly as she approached the bed.

Cameron watched as she leaned down and kissed the old man on the cheek. At the same time that he admired her emotional openness, he wondered why he hadn't been the first one to approach the bed and offer comfort.

Sometimes he despised his own coldness.

"Grandfather," he said, then took the elderly man's hand and squeezed it for a second. It felt far too frail and cool.

"Foolish...thing...to do," Julian muttered, struggling to keep his eyes open. Mrs. Monahan had told them he was on some sort of medication to keep him calm. The doctors had told her he could not afford to get so emotionally worked up over these things.

"Julian?" Michaela said, touching his forehead gently, smoothing back a lock of wintry white hair. "Don't talk. I don't want you to talk right now. I want you to listen."

His response was a smile.

Cameron watched her beautiful profile, watched the tears glistening in her eyes as she said, "We're getting married, Julian. Everything's fine, we worked it all out on the island."

The enormity of what she was doing hit him in the chest full force, and he could barely breathe.

He watched as Michaela moved the elderly man's hand and placed it on her slightly rounded abdomen.

"You simply have to be here when this baby is born," she whispered. "Mike's not around anymore, you know that."

Cameron watched, his throat tight, as a single tear slid down Julian's tired face.

He muttered something.

"What?" Michaela said, then moved closer so her face was next to his.

"So sorry... ultimatum."

"No." She tightened her grip on his hand, and Cameron watched, blinking against the moisture in his eyes, as she proceeded to scold his grandfather.

"No, you were right. We were both a pair of stubborn fools in the first place. All work, no play. You knew what you'd had with Mary, you told me that. It was no crime to want the same for Cameron."

"And... you," Julian whispered.

"Oh, don't say anything, Julian, I can't bear to see you hurt," Michaela whispered.

Cameron felt himself moving forward, clumsily putting his arm around her shoulders. She glanced up at him, surprised, then focused her concentration back on the frail, elderly man in the hospital bed.

"Always working, Julian. Who do you think he learned it from?" She nodded at Cameron.

Julian smiled then, and opened his eyes.

"I... need... your help, little girl."

She nodded, and Cameron watched the sudden, stubborn straightening of her shoulders. She still held his grandfather's hand cupped against her abdomen, but now there was an energy flowing through her that hadn't been there before.

"I'm going to nail this case for you, Julian. Do you know who Joshua Burrell has chosen for the trial?"

"Man named... Rawling."

"He's a vicious little twit, but not terribly bright. We can beat him."

"*You*... Want you... in court."

She hesitated, and Cameron knew why. Michaela's speciality was contract law, she hadn't been in a courtroom in a long time. He knew how frightening the prospect was, but he also knew she would move heaven and earth for his grandfather. Anything to see him get better.

"I'll be there, Julian." She took his hand and gently warmed it between her own. "There's just one thing. Is there anything you have, like notes, or a journal, or a letter, that would help us? Evidence that you created Bandit Bear?"

Cameron watched as his grandfather slowly opened his eyes. Once bright blue and twinkling with life, they were clouded with pain. But he still struggled to stay with them, and Cameron was subtly humbled by his relative's show of strength and spirit.

"The little house... the hideaway..."

"On the island," Cameron answered quickly, wanting his grandfather to know that he understood.

"Yes..."

"What are we looking for?" Cameron asked.

"Journal... bound in red leather... notes and... Mary's sketches. Get Manuel... to take you there..."

"Julian," Michaela said quietly. "We're going to take care of everything. You have absolutely nothing to worry about. We're your family, and we're going to take care of this once and for all."

"Take care... of... that baby."

"On my honor," she whispered.

He coughed then, and said, "Should have given you the company long ago, Cameron. But... I'm a foolish old man, as stubborn as... you are."

"Don't tire yourself," Cameron said, hurting for him.

Julian looked up at Michaela. "Don't let them... do this to me. Take away... my name. I don't... want it to end this way."

"I promise, Julian. You have my word. Besides, you have to get better to dance at my wedding." She leaned down and kissed the wrinkled cheek, then quietly walked out of the private room.

Cameron let her go, needing some time alone with the man who had been more than a grandfather to him.

"Told you," Julian muttered.

"What?" Cameron said, taking his grandfather's hand between his own, as Michaela had.

"One in a...million, that girl."

"I know," Cameron said softly. "I know."

HE FOUND HER in the corridor, on the pay phone.

Cameron leaned against the wall by the phone, letting it support his suddenly shaky legs. He wasn't sure why, but he had simply never been able to conceive of Julian dying. The old man had always had tremendous strength and vitality, but now Cameron could see that he should have taken the reins away from him a long time ago.

He blamed himself quickly, viciously, then let it go. Thinking of what might have been, should have been, was a complete waste of time. All they had was the present.

And a journal to find.

"He can't push the court date up like this!"

Michaela's irate voice was overloud for the hushed tones of the hospital. She slammed down the phone and turned toward him, her eyes flashing with anger. And he was reminded of the first time he'd seen her, when she had come striding into the office.

"I'd like to take Burrell and shove him off a cliff! First he fires me and now he pulls this!"

"Tell me."

"He's using Julian. He's going to leak nasty little tidbits to the press, make it a sensationalistic case, play it for all the publicity the firm can get!"

"Who told you this?"

"Cassandra. Her best girlfriend still works there."

"What about pushing up the date? What was that about?"

"Burrell is pushing to go to trial as soon as possible. How quickly can we get our hands on that journal?"

He lowered his voice, looking up and down the hospital corridor. A lawsuit like this one could ruin a company. Oh, not totally. Teddy's Toys would still make a tidy profit. But it was like a fast-food outlet that served spoiled sandwiches. Once you lost your name in something this ugly, it was hard to get back to where you'd been before.

"It's going to take a few days. I'll have to hike up to the cabin with my grandfather's friend, Manuel. Julian built the little house so that he and my grandmother could get away from it all, and it's really off the beaten track."

"I'm going with you—"

"No."

"Damn it, Cameron, I'm pregnant, not an invalid!"

"Julian told you to take care of that baby."

"A little exercise will do me a world of good—"

"The answer is no."

"The answer," she said, rising up on tiptoes and pushing her face right next to his, "is that you have no choice. You need a lawyer to go through the stuff in that house, because you need someone who's going to know what will hold up in court or what will make your grandfather look like he stole his own logo. That would break his heart, and you know it. So you don't have a choice, Cameron. You don't have a choice at all!"

THEY STOPPED briefly at Michaela's house to check on the cats, and let her pick up a few things for their trek into the heart of the island. Though Cameron still grumbled now and again about her accompanying him, Michaela knew she'd won this round.

She'd thought he was waiting downstairs, and thus when she caught a glimpse of him in the decorated nursery as she walked briskly down the hall, she stopped.

He was standing by the crib, his hand touching a mobile she'd hung over it. The mobile was a staple in the Teddy's Toys catalog, with brightly colored clowns and circus animals. When you wound it up, it played a tune.

"Cameron?" She knew they were on a tight schedule, and that he wanted to return to the airport as soon as possible.

"You did a good job," he said, his attention on the mobile as his touch made the tiny stuffed figures bob and sway.

"Thank you." She liked what she'd done with the room. It seemed to offer all the things she wanted the baby—their baby—to have. Love and protection and warmth.

"I meant... in the hospital room."

She'd already put that behind her. Emotionally, what she had told Julian had seemed like the right thing at the time. She'd had to give the old man something that had been in short supply in his expression. Hope.

"Oh. I was hoping you wouldn't be angry."

"I'm not."

"We can work it out later."

"I know."

"I didn't mean to back you into a corner—"

"I know, Mike. But I... wanted to thank you. I'm... not as good as you are with people."

She knew how proud he was, and how much that very private admission had cost him.

"You're welcome."

Silence filled the air around them, until she finally said, "I think we have a plane to catch."

He nodded, then stilled the mobile's movement with his hand.

THEIR FIRST step, after returning to Cameron's island, was to find Manuel.

"Manuel?" The shopkeeper squinted in the bright sunlight. "He never misses a cockfight. You'll find him over behind the Las Palmas tavern."

Teddy Bear Heir 165

Other island inhabitants were glad to share their various opinions, as well.

"Manuel? He's always out on his boat, that one. But how he can manage it is beyond me. Drinks a lot, you know?"

"Manuel? That lazy son of a gun owes me twenty dollars, and you tell him—"

"Manuel? I think he has a job as the lounge singer in that little hotel on the beach."

Thus, less than twenty-four hours after they'd left Julian's hospital room, both Cameron and Michaela found themselves in the smoky, dimly lit lounge of The Blue Parrot.

"'Fee-lee-ings... Nothing more than fee-lee-ings...'"

"Why is it," Michaela asked Cameron, "that they always sing that same song?"

"Must be something about playing to what the audience wants."

"But that song?"

"'Trying to for-get my fee-lings of lo-ove...'"

The scantily clad waitress, tugging the bodice of her sarong outfit up with one hand while she balanced their tray of drinks on the other, looked as tired as her feet in their six-inch heels probably felt.

"Is that Manuel on stage?" whispered Cameron as he gave the girl a generous tip.

She knew who he was. Everyone on the island knew who Cameron Black was. He'd bought the island, and taken its people from an incredibly poor standard of living to something considerably better. Julian had vacationed there years before Cameron had even been born, and relocated several of the Teddy's Toys factories to the island. Many of the women supplemented their family incomes by doing piecework and various other bits of sewing.

"That's Mannie. Jeez, you'd think he'd learn a few new tunes, wouldn't you?"

Michaela stuck her tongue out at Cameron behind her hand.

"When's his break coming up?" Cameron asked.

"Oh, twenty minutes or so."

"What does he drink?"

"Tequila shooters."

"What does the monkey drink?" Michaela asked as the waitress undulated away.

Cameron merely grimaced.

Manuel was on center stage, dressed in a rather worn tuxedo that had a glittery red collar and cuffs. Perched on the scratched piano, which was incongruously perfectly in tune, was a small brown monkey.

"'I wish I'd nev-ver met you gi-irl...'"

"He'd never make it in Vegas," she whispered before she took a sip of her Virgin Colada, and almost made Cameron laugh.

Strangely enough, when she'd made her various promises to Julian, all her fears had left her. What was left to be worried about when a man's life, reputation and entire career hung in the balance? How wrapped up could you be in your own problems when someone you cared for was in that much trouble? Women brought babies into the world every day. She'd manage.

When Manny's set ended, Cameron arranged for the waitress to deliver a bottle of Cuervo to his table, along with a shot glass.

The heavy-set Latin man looked around suspiciously, then visibly relaxed when he saw Cameron wave. He nodded his thanks, opened the bottle, and poured himself his first shot. The monkey sat to his left, happily engrossed in peeling a banana.

"I have a feeling," Cameron muttered as he stood, "that we'd better get the information while Manny's still standing."

"I don't know," said Michaela as she followed him around the tightly packed tables and chairs. "Everyone I've known who drank tequila never got drunk, and rarely had a hangover."

"With our luck," Cameron whispered back, "Manny won't even remember Julian's little hideaway."

But he did.

"Great place," he said, on his third shot. He'd unbuttoned his tuxedo, and his generous belly hung over his pants like the gentle ripples in a soft-serve ice-cream cone. "Used to take them up there all the time. Hard to find, but then, that's what they wanted. Privacy."

"Could you find it again?" Cameron questioned, and Michaela sensed his anxiety.

She'd never seen Cameron show his emotions before, or play them so close to the surface. Though both of them had slept sporadically on the flight back to the island, she could see that the idea of this travesty of a lawsuit having to go to an actual trial was weighing heavily on his mind.

"I could find it in a minute, if I didn't have a bum knee."

Michaela felt her heart start to sink. This couldn't be happening. Not when so much hung in the balance—

"But I used to take my son Perry up into the mountains. He could show you the way."

"Perry?" Michaela interrupted.

Manny smiled and poured himself another shot. "I know what you're thinking. It's not a very Spanish name. You see, I like to watch television. Made enough money singing in this lounge that I bought myself a satellite dish. And one of my favorite characters is that Perry Mason."

Michaela nodded her head. She wasn't even drinking tequila, and this was starting to make sense.

"You want to leave right away, *sí?*"

"*Sí.* Yes. As soon as possible." Cameron glanced around the smoky bar. "And we'd also like to keep this trip as quiet as possible. Our little secret, *comprende?*"

"Is your grandpapa in some sort of trouble?" Manny asked. His words weren't slurred after six shots, and genuine concern etched his expression.

"Yes. We need to get to that little hideaway he built as quickly as possible."

"Okay, Mr. Cameron. I will have both Perry and Barnaby at your house first thing in the morning."

NEITHER of them slept that well that evening. It was a hot, sultry, tropical night, with the promise of rain, so they both stayed out on one of the large balconies, each in their own hammock.

"I guess his kids should be grateful he wasn't real fond of 'Gilligan's Island,'" Michaela remarked, taking another sip of her ice tea.

"You don't know that. Last thing I heard, Manny had thirteen children by three different wives."

"Must be that island air."

She was deliberately keeping clear of him. She'd been careful not to brush up against him or accidently touch him during the entire time they'd talked to Manny, or all the way home. Now, in separate hammocks, she felt relatively safe. And she was certain of one thing. Cameron would never use any kind of force or coercion on her.

"That guy sure liked to tell stories," Cameron muttered. His voice sounded vaguely disembodied in the tropical darkness.

"Yeah, but he enjoyed them so much, it was hard not to go along with him."

"He'd make more money telling stories than singing those songs."

"Sort of a Garrison Kieller of the tropics."

He choked on his drink, and she smiled into the darkness. She'd been able to make him laugh before. Before *L'affaire d'hôtel*. Actually, before *Le Discov-*

erie de le Bébé. Maybe it would be possible to build from there.

It wasn't exactly that she didn't have enough energy to deal with two things at once. It was simply that she wanted to turn all her energy toward getting Julian out of trouble before she concentrated on her own. He'd helped her in so many ways, especially right after her father had died. And she genuinely liked Julian, and couldn't bear to see him in such trouble and anxiety.

"Got your vitamins packed?"

"Yes. Boy, now I know why I tried to keep this pregnancy a secret."

If a smile could be heard in the darkness, she heard his.

"Am I that bad?"

"It's not bad. Not exactly. It's just— Well, you can be a nag. At times."

"I suppose I can. But it's only—"

"For my own good. I know. Pop used to run that one by me at least once a week."

They were silent for a moment. Then he asked, "Do you miss him?"

"All the time."

"I met him once," Cameron said lazily. "Julian gave a party and invited him. I don't remember how they knew each other."

"They met at a policemen's benefit for battered children. Julian donated the toys for a children's center."

"That's right."

"They liked each other."

"Yeah, they did."

"I liked him."

"So did I."

Silence reigned for a short time, but it was comfortable.

"Mike? You asleep?"

"No."

"It's going to be a hard trip—"

"You are *not* leaving me behind."

"No. I just want you to promise me that if it gets to be too much, you'll make sure and tell us to stop. So you can rest."

"Why don't we ask Barnaby and Perry to see if Mork and Mindy can come along and carry me in some sort of litter? Or perhaps, at this late time and date, we could rent an elephant caravan?"

He didn't laugh. "There must be a place that rents horses. Maybe we could—"

"Stop. No. We don't have time. Julian's reputation and entire company can't wait till we scour the village."

"But he wouldn't want you to lose this baby."

She took a deep breath, knowing she was going to get herself in trouble. "What about you, Cameron? Would you be relieved if something happened to the baby?"

"What the hell kind of question is that?"

She didn't answer.

He swung up out of the hammock, then walked over to where she lay in hers and looked down at her.

Moonlight lit his face. And the beauty of it still affected her to her core.

"I'm going to put that remark down to hormonal crazies."

She didn't say anything, just looked up at him. Her eyes widened as he bent over her hammock and took her lips in a short, fierce, aggressive kiss that ended just as her anger faded and she began to want more.

"What was that for?" she whispered. His face was so close to hers, she could have counted his eyelashes if she'd wanted to.

"That," he whispered, "was to let you know that I haven't forgotten about us. And as soon as this entire thing is settled, you and I are going to have to settle us."

She wrinkled her nose and he kissed it.

She put her hand behind his neck and pulled him down for another kiss.

He obliged.

She forgot all about why she was mad at him, why he was mad at her. She forgot it all in the sexual blaze that kindled and caught so easily between the two of them.

He'd unbuttoned her blouse and had cupped her bare breast in his hand when he suddenly straightened and backed away. She lay in the hammock, stunned with sensuality, and simply looked up at him.

She felt drugged, as if she couldn't move, could only respond to him.

"Why are you going away?" she finally whispered.

"Because, Mike, we're going on one hell of a hike tomorrow morning. And if I keep this up, you won't be able to stand up at dawn, let alone walk."

She threw a pillow at his departing back, then covered her ears against the sound of his soft laughter.

Chapter Nine

They started at dawn.

In the pouring rain.

Michaela was determined not to complain and, unless her or especially the baby's health was at stake, not to slow down their party. She fell in line behind Perry, Cameron and Barnaby. Baretta brought up the rear.

It touched her how Manny had insisted that three of his sons accompany them. Perry was by far the most knowledgeable, and an excellent trail guide.

The tropical island seemed like any other when she looked at the expanses of shimmery beaches, swaying palm trees and glistening water. But once they headed toward the interior, and up into the mountainous region, it was a different country altogether.

She couldn't really tell what time of day it was, because she couldn't see the sun. Thick green foliage obscured the sunlight, and the rain that fell was warm and soft. She'd dressed in long khaki pants and a long-sleeved, cotton top, and even though she was soaked, she wasn't uncomfortable. The top of her head was covered with a white canvas baseball cap, and she'd pulled back her hair into a short ponytail at the nape of her neck.

All in all, she decided to comport herself like her heroine from the world of the movies, Katherine Hepburn. She wouldn't complain. This little hike into the island's interior would be a piece of cake for a woman who still swam in the Atlantic Ocean, in the winter, in her eighties.

She'd been so nervous about starting with the rest of them, she hadn't even had morning sickness. But she'd packed enough packages of salted crackers and flat breads in her backpack to stock a small café. That, and about fifteen pairs of underwear. If she had enough crackers and underwear, she could get through anything.

Birds shrieked in the trees, and the most incredible flowers glistened with moisture. One in particular, a brilliant shade of red, almost cried out for her to pick it.

She started to give in to temptation.

And felt a hand on her arm.

Looking back, she saw Baretta's calm expression. The youngest of Manny's boys was only about sixteen, but he had the expression and bearing of an older man.

He shook his head.

Comprehension dawned in a heartbeat.

"Endangered species?"

"Nope. Poison."

"Aha!" She moved away from the beautiful bloom with lightning speed and fell into line behind Barnaby.

They stopped for lunch by a waterfall, and she discreetly asked Baretta to find her a place she could relieve herself without running into any more poisonous foliage.

"Okay," he said cheerfully. "I checked it all out. No snakes or spiders."

"Snakes or spiders?" she said carefully, steadying herself against a vine-covered tree as her heart picked up speed.

"You okay, Mike?" called Cameron.

What would Hepburn do?

"Fine. Fine." No mere snake or spider would get in the way of Kate the Great. She smiled gamely at Cameron, and darted around the tree, then around another, until she found the exact spot that Baretta had scoped out for her.

After a lunch of some actually rather terrific sandwiches that Cameron's dour-faced cook had prepared for them, they sat for a quarter of an hour, then resumed their journey.

Had she had the breath, and had her legs not felt like two-ton weights, Michaela would have enjoyed her surroundings. As it was, she was struggling to keep up. Her daily aerobics class hadn't prepared her for this stint in what seemed a never-ending Bomba of the Jungle movie.

"Look!" Baretta said beneath his breath.

Teddy Bear Heir   177

She glanced over and saw the cutest little bird sitting on the branch of an immense tree. Its plumage was bright and fluffy, and the bird cocked its little head at her. She wondered if it was about to break into song.

"It's darling!"

Baretta grinned. "That bird, she pecks you, you're history."

She could feel her smile fading. "Poisonous?"

"Nah, not really. You'd probably run a really high fever and feel like hell for about a month afterward. Sort of like the Changa spider—"

And Baretta regaled her with tales of the various flora and fauna of the jungle. Michaela heard none of them.

Her every thought was focused on encountering as few of them as possible. On getting Julian's journals... and getting out.

WHY DOES he have to look like he's in his element? she wondered crossly as they ate dinner that evening. Cameron had never looked so handsome. He was dressed in faded jeans, boots and a khaki shirt. She could see where he had a knife strapped to his side, and even detected the bulge of a gun in the back waistband of his pants.

Cameron of the Jungle.

Mr. Control goes on a wilderness expedition.

He was really enjoying himself, talking and laughing with Manny's sons, gesturing and speaking rapidly in Spanish. And as her command of the language had never been that good, she simply smiled and nodded and pretended she was having a wonderful time.

Evening couldn't come soon enough for her.

"BUT WHERE am I going to sleep?"

Cameron ran his hands through his hair in frustration.

"This isn't my idea of a joke, Mike. The boys assumed we were married, so they only brought two tents with them."

"But I can't sleep with you!" she whispered.

"I don't remember asking. But it's either with me or with the boys. Baretta actually seems rather fond of you."

The look she gave him was more eloquent than any word that sprang to mind. And plenty of them sprang.

"You could sleep with Perry, Barnaby and Baretta. If you were a real gentleman."

"I'm not, and their tent won't sleep four."

She glanced from tent to tent, weighing her options. Cameron, sensing her hesitation, turned and ducked down, entering his tent. She stood outside and wondered what to do while, as if on cue, a light film of rain started to come down, clinging to her hat, hair and clothing in tiny, shining little drops.

"It's raining," she called.

He came out of their tent. "I'll put up some sort of makeshift hammock," he said, his voice sharp with frustration and annoyance.

"Thank you. I knew you were really a gentleman." She walked past him and entered their tent.

Fifteen minutes later she was beyond caring what Katherine Hepburn would have done, *African Queen* or not.

"Cameron?"

"What?"

"There's a spider in the tent."

"Squash it." His tone was ruthless.

"It's pretty big."

"I thought you didn't want me in the tent."

"I didn't but— Ah!"

She came out of the tent in a flash, and he swung down out of his makeshift hammock and walked lazily over to the tent.

"Where?"

"Inside."

He sighed. "I know that. Give me a general idea of the vicinity."

"Up by the pillow on that side." She pointed.

He took hold of her upper arms. "If I shouldn't make it back, tell Julian I did my best."

She punched his arm. "Just kill it!"

He came back out within minutes, mission accomplished. Manny's three sons had already retired for the night, so now they stood in the middle of the dark tropical jungle—alone.

"Get in that tent." The look in his eyes brooked no argument.

As she started to comply, she realized he was following her.

"Don't say it. I'm not spending the night out in that hammock so you can wake me up every time you hear a noise, see a bug or feel a snake."

"Ho-ho, what a Freudian slip." But she didn't protest when he followed her into the tent or lay down on the sleeping bag next to hers.

They lay in silence for several minutes before she spoke.

"Cameron?"

"What?"

"Thanks for killing the spider."

"It's okay. It was pretty big."

"Well, I wouldn't be afraid of any old spider. There are plenty of those in the garden at home, and I just stay out of their way."

"No, this one was pretty impressive."

They both lay quietly for a while.

"Cameron?"

"What?"

"Thanks for taking me along. I really am having a good time, in a perverse kind of way."

"Good. How are you feeling?"

"Good."

"Did you take your—"

"Yes. With breakfast."

"Any morning sickness?"

"I'm too exhausted to throw up."

"Try to get some sleep. We have another long day tomorrow."

Silence.

"Cameron?"

"What?"

"Did you hear that noise?"

"No."

"It sounded like... drums or something."

"There are no lost tribes on this island. No head hunters, no cannibals, no pygmies, no forms of alien life, no pod people, nothing."

"You're sure?"

"Positive. Come here, I'm going to distract you."

"Oh, no—"

"A little closer—"

"My legs feel like lead weights!"

"You won't need to move them."

What was dangerous inside the tent was infinitely preferable to anything outside. She didn't resist as he moved closer, taking her into the shelter of his arms and lowering his face toward hers. At that last instant, before he kissed her, she wondered how she'd been able to hold out this long.

He broke the kiss. "It's dark, just like last time," he whispered.

She blushed at the memory of that darkened suite at the Four Seasons. At the memory of the king-size bed. And the wild, passionate abandon they'd shared in it.

"You're taking advantage of me."

"I know. It's shameless." His hand skimmed over her cotton shirt and slowly pulled it out of her waistband. She felt the warmth of his hand come slowly up her back, then she realized his hands were around her waist, dangerously close to her breasts.

"Cameron, I..."

"Kiss me again."

She did.

"What were you thinking?" he whispered, his lips close to her ear. "What were you thinking that night, right before I started to make love to you?"

She couldn't speak, she was so unbearably excited. He'd eased her cotton top up past her breasts, and she pulled it up over her head, shrugging out of it.

She felt secure when she packed underwear and, knowing Cameron was going to be on this particular trip, she'd packed some pretty spectacular underwear. It was her secret mission in life, to make Mr. Control lose control.

The black lace bra was exquisite, and even though there was hardly any light in the tent at all, he traced the design with his fingers, over and over her sensitive skin.

"Pretty," he murmured, then kissed her on the neck, beneath her ear. She shivered.

"Take it off for me," he whispered.

She was beyond caring, beyond thinking about consequences. She wanted to please him. She wanted the pleasure he was capable of giving her. Life had been hard for both of them, and she wanted to forget, to stop thinking for a while. To feel.

She unsnapped the fastening of her bra, and was suddenly glad they were both concealed in darkness. The changes pregnancy had caused in her body made her feel self-conscious, and she knew it would be easier, this first time with him, in the dark.

She needn't have worried. His hands shaped her upper body, pleasuring her, pleasuring him, remembering. Somehow, it was more erotic in the dark when she couldn't see his face. He shifted, and she cried out softly as he began to kiss his way down her neck, to her shoulders, then down to her breasts.

They were agonizingly full and sensitive. And he was so gentle, just barely touching them, touching them just enough to send her into a maelstrom of shivering pleasure.

"Beautiful," he whispered, kissing them, softly testing their weight and feel. "So beautiful."

She trembled in his arms. They were lying side by side, his arms were around her, she couldn't have moved if a dozen spiders had suddenly invaded the tent. She could only feel his touch, hear his voice. Respond.

He moved over her, easing her onto her back, bracing his weight on his elbows. He took her breasts into his mouth, first one nipple, then the other, making them feel fuller and heavier, making her nipples harden unbearably. Brushing them softly with his tongue, caressing them with his lips.

Vaguely, in the back of her head, she realized he was lowering the zipper of her khaki trousers.

"I thought," she whispered, trying not to let her voice shake, "you said I wouldn't have to move my legs?"

"I'll carry you piggyback tomorrow," he muttered, pushing the material down, past her waist and around her lower legs. Before he even had her pants all the way off, his hand was between her legs, seeking.

She couldn't lie to him. Her body refused to comply with her mind's mischief. He found the hot wetness between her legs and she heard his satisfaction in the rough, masculine moan he gave as he slid his fingers inside her, then lowered his head toward the cradle of her thighs.

He pushed at one leg with his palm, and she bent it at the knee, giving him greater access to what he sought even though her pants were still tangled around her ankles. He found her with his mouth, and the sensation was so exquisite she arched off the sleeping bag and cried out. Then she felt his hand over her mouth, muffling her cries as he made love to her. He built her pleasure slowly, using lips and tongue and hand, until she was writhing mindlessly, helplessly, against the ground.

Only when he felt those familiar feminine contractions did he let her go, sliding slowly down her body, unlacing her boots, slipping them off, then sliding her pants the rest of the way down.

She was totally naked and she didn't even care. Totally naked in a world of snakes and spiders, poisonous birds and plants, and all she could think about was getting him inside her.

It seemed to be all he could think about, because she heard the rasp of his zipper in the dark stillness of the tent.

She reached for him, sliding her hand inside the opening, cupping him, stroking the hard, impatient masculine flesh. She smiled as she heard his groan, then helped him push his worn jeans down over his hips and down his thighs until he finally kicked both boots and pants off at the foot of their makeshift bed.

She lay back down on her side and he joined her.

"This is crazy," she whispered, kissing him, his mouth, his neck, his eyes.

"This," he whispered back, "is absolutely right."

She touched him, stroked him, kissed him until he rolled her onto her back and braced his weight with his elbows.

"Tell me if I hurt you," he whispered hoarsely, and something in her heart melted at the thought of his exerting such control for her, thinking of protecting her at the moment at which he could have taken his greatest pleasure.

"You won't," she assured him.

"Tell me," he whispered as he found her, opened her, penetrated with a careful, shallow stroke.

She pressed her hands into the small of his back and encouraged him on.

"More," she whispered.

He groaned, and held on to his control by the sheerest of threads.

She kissed him, then bit his lip. "More."

He gave her what she wanted.

Within a very short time, he was embedded completely inside her, holding himself very still, kissing her as she kissed him back and wrapped her legs around his hips.

He moved, and the pleasure was so great she bit his shoulder so as not to cry out and wake the three people she knew for miles around. He made love to her and it was the same as that first night, but now she loved him even more because she carried his child.

He rolled over onto the sleeping bags, taking her with him, letting her straddle his body and set their pace.

She knew it was his way of ensuring that he wouldn't hurt her, and was touched by his caring so very much. She sat astride him, her hair falling over her face, her hands against his chest. Then she lay down on him, pressing herself against him as she had that first night, so long ago.

She moved on him, taking him in, deeply, fully, then moved again, unsheathing his full erection. This time he was the one who groaned.

She knew the signs as his large body stiffened and his muscles tensed even more beneath her.

"I want you," she whispered.

He shuddered.

"I need you." She lowered her face to his and bit his earlobe, moving the entire time.

I love you, she thought, not wanting to say it as his oh-so-knowing fingers moved to where they were joined and started her on her final climax. She cried out and her contractions started his. He seemed to burst inside her, so strongly, his hands gripping her buttocks with punishing force. She could faintly make out his shape in the confines of the dark tent, his head thrown back, his neck arched.

He cried out as he found his release, and she found it beautiful.

THE FOLLOWING morning, when her muscles protested and refused to work, she didn't find anything about the entire experience beautiful.

She'd known it was going to be a bad day when she'd woken up just before dawn, grabbed Cameron's khaki shirt, slipped it on, then raced out the front of the tent and thrown up.

Off to the side, of course. If it was possible for a woman to be imminently practical about vomiting, then she was that woman.

He was beside her in an instant, dressed in his unsnapped jeans, holding her head.

"I'm sorry," she muttered afterward as he handed her a paper towel. "I'm sorry."

"Don't." He steered her back inside the tent and made her lie down. "I'll talk to Perry and see if we can start just a little later—"

"No! I'll keep up, I don't want to slow things down because—"

Cameron put his hand underneath her chin and tilted her head up so she had to face him.

"As I believe I heard someone say once, it's my way or the highway."

She believed him.

They remained in camp that morning. He brought her some soup, which she refused. Instead she munched a few crackers and lay back down.

Cameron stayed by her side and finished the soup.

"How many days did Perry say it would take to reach Julian's house?"

"Two and a half. Maybe three."

"So maybe this could be our half day, and we won't lose that much time."

"Don't worry," he said as he cleaned up the cracker wrappers she'd wadded up into a small ball. "We'll get there."

She willed herself to stop feeling queasy by lunchtime, and after they'd all eaten a light meal and broken camp, they were on their way.

THE ISLAND terrain had leveled out for a stretch, and Michaela actually found herself enjoying their journey for large stretches at a time.

Kate the Great, that's me.

Until they reached what Perry quaintly referred to as "The Gate to the Heavens."

"What does that mean?" she asked, hooking her fingers into the back of Cameron's belt as they walked along the jungle trail. She was careful to avoid his gun.

Perry grinned, his teeth startlingly white against his tanned face. It was clear he loved the outdoor life.

"It's a bridge that spans a huge—how do you say?—gorge. We have to cross it in order to climb the second hill."

"Which Perry assures me is not anywhere as steep as the first," Cameron added soothingly.

"Bridge? Gorge?" She felt her own rising sharply and reached for another package of crackers. "What kind of material is this bridge made out of?"

"It's safe, *señora*," Baretta assured her.

What did he know? He actually seemed to like all the poisonous reptiles and birds in this jungle, not to mention his fondness for snakes.

"That one, for instance," he'd said just that morning, pointing to a tiny green snake hanging from a tree branch off to the side of the trail. "If he bites you, you go into a fit and maybe die."

If she had to cross that bridge, going into a fit and dying sounded better and better. She hadn't bothered to tell Cameron about her total fear of heights, because she'd thought they would simply be walking along jungle trails. She didn't know this little trip included a few scenes right out of *Cliffhanger*.

As much as she liked Sylvester Stallone, she'd watched the entire movie through her fingers. Her imagination ran riot as she thought of what lay ahead.

HER IMAGINATION hadn't even come close.

"You see, *señora*? It is just a little rope bridge, but quite sturdy. You would have to shake it quite hard to get it to come down, and we will not do that, yes?"

"But it sort of...*sways* when you walk on it."

"*Sí*," said Barnaby. "But you don't stop, you don't fall off."

"I'll go first," said Baretta cheerfully.

Be my guest.

He loped across the narrow bridge, as nimble as a mountain goat, as quick as one of those damn poisonous snakes.

"Now I go," said Barnaby.

Cameron nodded. He was watching her closely, and she didn't like the look on his face. No wonder she'd chosen to make love to this man—*twice*, now—in the dark. Those eyes saw too much.

"Now you, Mr. Cameron?" asked Perry.

"Now Mike goes."

The moment of truth. *What would Kate do?*
The hell with Kate. She groveled.

"Please, Cameron, don't make me." At the moment, Julian, the trial back in San Francisco, the journal, all were forgotten in her desperate fear of walking across that bridge.

"You're going to hold on to me, we're going to cross that bridge together. Come on, Mike, I know you can do it."

"I saw that scene in the Stallone movie where he reached for the girl's glove after the snap broke, and she fell. And I know it was done with computer effects but— Oh, God, Cameron, this is real and I don't think—"

"Take hold of my belt."

She was almost hysterical as he took her hand and placed it on his belt. He was in front, she was looking at his back, and he started toward a bridge that looked like something a first grader might have made out of Popsicle sticks.

"Please, don't make me..."

He turned, then cupped her face in his hands.

"I can't leave you here, Mike. And we can't stop now. I want you to follow me, follow right behind me, and don't look down."

Don't look down.

She remembered his command until they got to the middle of the bridge.

She looked down.

She stopped. She froze. She couldn't move.

"Damn it, Mike."

Everything suddenly became totally clear.

"I want you to leave me here, Cameron. Go on, I'll be fine."

"Then Perry won't be able to get across."

He could make jokes at a time like this?

She snapped.

"I do have my hand in a very convenient position to your gun."

"Damn it, Mike, I'm faster than you are. Now move those legs or I'll shoot you myself."

"I can't."

"Look at my back."

"Cameron—"

"Look at my back."

She did. Somehow, a couple of hundred feet above a steep jungle gorge, on a bridge that was probably sixty feet long and only a few feet wide, she found the inner strength and fortitude to stop looking down and concentrate on Cameron's back.

Well, it wasn't inner strength and fortitude, exactly. He sounded awfully serious about the gun thing, and she suddenly realized that she didn't want to die.

The wind whipped up and the rope bridge jerked alarmingly. She screamed and went down on her knees, so ashamed of being a coward but not knowing how to get away from a fear so overpowering it almost consumed her.

"Mike. Mike."

It seemed a long time later when she finally heard his voice.

"Mike."

"Cameron?" Her own voice was quavery and filled with tears.

"Mike, I want you to keep your eyes closed and stand up. Slowly."

"I never should have come along on this trip!"

"Let's argue over that one later. Now, can you stand up if you keep your eyes closed?"

"I think so..."

He talked to her the entire time, walking for both of them as she kept her one hand firmly around his leather belt and used the other to keep her balance on the shaky bridge.

"Just a few more feet, Mike, and we'll be there. A few more feet, a few more feet..."

She felt his arms around her and then he was swinging her onto solid ground. She felt like laughing and crying at the same time, which was exactly what she did as she kept her arms around his neck in a stranglehold.

He lowered her to the ground and held her in his lap as Perry, Barnaby and Baretta stood a discreet distance away.

"Oh, Cameron. Oh, my God. Oh, God—"

He kissed her forehead. "Any other phobias I should know about?"

"What?"

"Oh, you know, snakes and heights and things like that."

She wiped away her tears with the back of her hand and leaned against his chest, reassured by the steady beat of his heart. "I'm not crazy about thunderstorms. Lightning and that sort of thing."

He nodded, then kissed the top of her head.

"I cannot stand heights, Cameron. I just can't."

"Okay."

She turned her head and kissed him, so happy to be on solid ground she was almost dizzy with it. Then she placed her fingers against his lips and whispered something that made him smile.

"But I'm not afraid of the dark."

Chapter Ten

They reached Julian's hideaway right on schedule, and as Michaela stepped out into the clearing and saw the structure, she almost laughed out loud.

A little hideaway. Sure.

It was like saying that Madonna had a little money.

The house was low and close to the ground, but it covered a considerable amount of it. A one-story structure, it had been built to blend in to the tropical jungle surroundings. It was airy and open and really quite beautiful, the actual building surrounding an open courtyard.

She'd been expecting a cabin in the woods, a one-room structure, a tin roof. But this looked like a spacious bungalow at a major resort. There was room enough for a dozen people in this house. A dozen large people.

She'd never figure rich people out.

It was charming inside, as well, and for the first time she had a sense of the enormity of Julian's loss when Mary had died. The decor was rather whimsical, but it was a home. Toys of all sorts adorned shelves, along with books and small sculptures. Framed prints graced the walls and several wall hangings added brilliant splashes of color against the cool, white stucco walls.

They'd left the main door open and a small green lizard darted in, ran halfway up one of the walls, saw them, and disappeared down the hallway.

She glanced at Baretta, and he grinned at her reassuringly.

"That one's okay. No poison."

They'd set all their equipment down in the large foyer and she heard Perry, Barnaby and Baretta talking excitedly with Cameron. It was decided that their guides would have the next twenty-four hours off, to do what they wanted to do, which seemed to be just lie about and enjoy themselves. They'd stayed in the guest quarters before, and within the half hour had left for the far end of the hideaway.

That left Michaela alone with Cameron.

She didn't mind. Something had changed during this expedition, something she couldn't really articulate, but had made her feel better about their chances as a couple. Now, with work to do and a decided time limit, they didn't really have the luxury of being able to hash it all out.

"Where did he say the journal would be?" she asked him.

"Somewhere among all the books. He wasn't really sure where."

She glanced around at the large living room. Books lined the shelves from floor to ceiling.

When she had thought of the hideaway, she'd thought of a tiny, tin-roofed shack, with the journal on a dusty little table in the middle of the room. Like in those movies where the adventurer opens the door and a shaft of sunlight spills over the object he seeks.

No such luck here.

"Well, I'll start at this end and you can take the other," she said.

"Mike, don't you think you should rest a little? I mean, the baby and... and all..."

Michaela looked in his eyes and they somehow seemed softer, like his voice. The steeliness that had gleamed there when they'd argued on the rickety footbridge had disappeared. In its place was... Concern. Affection.

Maybe even a touch of fear. For her and their baby.

Yes, maybe this trip would *help them.*

She grinned up at him. "You'd better take advantage of the moments I feel this terrific." She patted his butt. "Now, get to work."

THEY WERE HOT, dusty and covered with sweat, and hours later, still no closer to Julian's elusive journal than they'd been in San Francisco.

"Maybe if we called Mrs. Monahan—"

"I already did," Cameron said, pulling another leather-bound volume off the bookcase, flipping it open and examining its contents. He put it back on the shelf and continued searching. "She's asked him a few times, but his mind seems a little muddled."

"Probably all the stress he's been under," she muttered, reaching for another volume.

She found a journal, later that afternoon, but it was Mary's. Closing it after reading only enough to ascertain it wasn't Julian's and had none of the information she sought, Michaela slid it carefully back onto the shelf, then glanced over at Cameron.

He was hard at work.

How had two people who had so obviously loved each other and been able to commit to each other made it possible for Cameron to harbor such fears? For she knew it was fear, and would have realized this even if Julian hadn't talked to her that evening on the jet.

What had really happened to make him feel the way he did? Many children lost their parents, yet went on to become adults and raise families of their own.

She continued to work as she thought, sliding out volume after volume, checking title after title.

From what Julian had told her, she had the impression that Cameron had loved his parents very much, but that their jet-setting life-style hadn't had much room in it for a child. He'd been five years old, without brothers and sisters, when they had died. Five years old and all alone.

Except for Julian and Mary.

She glanced up at the journal she'd so recently put back on the shelf—Mary's journal—and wondered if there were any clues inside that leather-bound volume.

Don't even think about it.

Sighing, and brushing her damp hair off her forehead, she got back to work.

CAMERON WATCHED her as they worked, watched her as unobtrusively as possible. Though there were fans placed strategically on tables and even on the ceilings, the weather was still hot and muggy. Julian had never cared for air-conditioning in this particular house, so fans had been his choice. And though they moved the air, the air itself was still tropically muggy.

He smiled as the little green lizard darted into the room, close to Michaela's feet. She looked down, saw the little reptile, and didn't even flinch.

Cameron still felt bad about the incident at the bridge. He hadn't meant to push her that hard, but he really hadn't known what else to do. They couldn't have turned back, she wouldn't have made it on foot, retracing their trail to his house by the beach, without going through major exhaustion.

Here, once they found the journal, he could arrange to have them picked up by helicopter. He'd set off a few carefully placed flares, call one of the pilots on the island that he trusted, and have them back at the jet and on their way to San Francisco in no time.

That is, if they could find the journal and Julian's notes about Bandit Bear.

"Have you found any of Mary's journals?" he called out, sliding yet another book out of its slot on the wooden shelf.

"One."

"Set them down on the table. She did a lot of sketching for Julian, we might be able to find something in it to support our case."

They stopped for a quick supper, eating in the spacious, fully equipped kitchen.

"Boy, Julian certainly didn't believe in roughing it, did he?"

"His idea of luxury was no phones, no television, absolutely no contact with the outside world. He liked coming up here with Mary and 'recharging the spirit.' Those were his exact words."

He was right. She already felt energized, after only a few hours in this tropical oasis.

Somehow things seemed more relaxed, despite the importance of what they were here for. Cameron, too, must have felt it. Since they'd arrived at the hideaway, he was talking more. And she never knew how much she'd missed talking to him.

Not about contracts and partnerships, but about life.

She could have sat there for hours with him, listening to his stories about Julian and Mary. But there was work to be done, so they resumed their search of the dusty volumes.

It was almost midnight before they found it.

"Cameron," Michaela said quietly, her anticipation so great her hands were shaking as she clutched a small red leather-bound book.

He glanced up while listening on the cellular phone. From the moment they had started this trip, he'd remained in constant contact with Mrs. Monahan concerning Julian's health.

"I think I found it."

IT WAS Julian's journal, and as she sat at the table in the master bedroom and read, Michaela's sense of anticipation and relief grew. They not only had a case here, they had one so cut-and-dried that Coleman, Watts and Burrell were going to look like a bunch of greedy, publicity-hungry fools.

In other words, exactly what they were.

It fascinated her, reading about the early years of Teddy's Toys. Julian's dreams, his absolute and unwavering vision came alive on the page, along with the story of his great love for his wife, Mary.

Both of them had loved children, and the tragedy of their marriage had been the fact that Mary had been physically unable to have more than one child. But they had spread their love for children throughout the world, through Teddy's Toys.

There were several passages in Julian's fine, careful handwriting concerning his love for his wife that had Michaela reaching for a box of tissues.

"What?" Cameron asked once, and she started. She'd been so involved in Julian and Mary's world, the early years of their marriage, that she'd almost forgotten where she was.

She blew her nose again, not even glancing at him, she was so absorbed in the material. "Oh, it's just the way he loved her. The way they cared for each other."

Not noticing the expression on his face, she continued reading far into the night.

HE WATCHED her as he worked, and knew he was falling in love all over again. And he wondered at the fact that he had spent most of his life consciously trying to shy away from that most complex and dangerous of emotions.

He'd learned, early on, that life wasn't always fair. And he'd picked himself up and gotten on with it. His parents' deaths had been traumatic, but living with his grandparents had been something of a relief. He'd always felt safer with them, as if he could really be a child as opposed to a little adult.

He'd adored his grandmother, and her death when he'd been in his early thirties had shaken him far more than losing either of his parents.

He'd also seen what it had done to Julian.

Julian, who had lived and breathed and been Teddy's Toys, had gone on an emotional rampage. He'd left the company, and Cameron had found himself making all the executive decisions in his grandfather's absence. Finally, when he'd managed to arrange a little time off, he'd flown to the island, knowing where his grandfather had probably chosen to hide and grieve.

He'd been right.

He'd only been up to the hideaway once before, and that had been by helicopter. They'd dropped him into the jungle not far from the house, and he'd hiked the last quarter mile.

And found Julian completely emotionally destroyed.

His grandfather, who had never left the house without looking immaculate, his grandfather, who had never, ever revealed by word or deed a single violent emotion, his grandfather, who possessed one of the most optimistic spirits on the planet, had been sitting on the balcony with a bottle of Scotch, contemplating ending his own life.

Cameron had never forgotten the time he'd spent, talking, cajoling, bullying. And in a way, his fate had been fitting, for his grandfather had slowly brought him back to life after his parents had died, and he was returning the emotional favor.

It had taken him almost a week. A week of constant watching, a week of continual talking, a week of drawing on a faith he hadn't even been sure he possessed at the start. But finally he had managed to convince Julian to go on, and the two of them had been picked up, flown to the house by the beach, and then on to the San Francisco office.

The next time he'd seen his grandfather, his hair and beard had been neatly trimmed and he was dressed impeccably in one of his many business suits. He'd been chairing a crucial board meeting as if he'd never been away.

And that year he'd given close to a million dollars to Mary's favorite charity, which helped orphanages all over the world.

He'd thrown himself back into his work, and only Cameron had been able to see that a part of the old man was missing. His heart.

To love like that and lose it all? Not for him.

He'd never been aware of making a conscious decision, but after that episode with his grandfather he'd put a lot more energy into quantity as far as his relationships with the opposite sex went. Not for him, the horrible agony he'd seen on Julian's face. Not for him, even the contemplation of ending it all over another person.

Later, he'd talked with Julian about their week in the jungle.

"It was a selfish thing to do," Julian said, looking him directly in the eye. "Imagine my leaving you that way. It doesn't bear thinking about."

"But you were going to do it. You wanted to," he argued.

"I wasn't thinking real straight right about then," Julian said, and sighed. "I wasn't thinking at all."

Now, in the master bedroom of the same house in which he'd seen his grandfather reach the lowest point of his life, he looked at Michaela and realized that he was lost.

It didn't matter what he did. It didn't matter where he went, or what happened, or how much he tried to deny it.

He loved her. In a way he'd never loved anyone else.

Now, more than ever before, he understood what had driven Julian during those dark days. He understood the look of utter despair his grandfather had first shot at him when he'd stepped onto the balcony and found a filthy old man clutching a bottle of Scotch as if it were his only friend in the world.

He understood the rage that had propelled him to take apart an entire room in one of the Teddy's Toys' factories because the little llama didn't look the way Mary had sketched it.

He understood why Julian had placed so much importance on love. Because no matter how much it scared him—the potential of being torn apart that way—in the end, it was the only thing that made life bearable.

He thought of telling Mike all this as she pored over Julian's journal, occasionally stopping to make notes on a yellow legal pad.

Hell, he even loved the way she bit her tongue while she worked, so that just the tiniest tip of it showed between her lips. She'd argue with him, and deny it, and he found himself looking forward to it.

That's how he knew he was crazy. A goner, pure and simple.

But he didn't want to tell her right now. He wanted a time and a place that were better for something like a declaration of love. He wanted a quiet time in their lives so that both of them might cherish this particular memory.

A wife and a child. Two things he'd thought he'd never have. Two things he'd argued with Julian about, thinking the old man a fool.

Julian was quite possibly the wisest man he'd ever known.

Teddy Bear Heir 205

He was startled out of his thoughts by the sound of Michaela snapping the journal shut. He glanced up at her.

"I've got it. It's all here. We're going to win."

He rose then, and walked over to the table, taking her by the hand, pulling her up and out of the chair and into his arms. He enfolded her in his embrace, and felt the surprised stiffening of her body as she first realized what he was doing.

And then she melted against him, her cheek resting on his chest. He found that he liked the way she fit in his arms, against him. Couldn't think of anyone else he wanted to hold like this.

Close to his heart for the rest of his life.

THEY PHONED Mrs. Monahan with the good news, then Cameron arranged for a pilot to pick them up. They agreed on a time and general location.

"Thank God," Michaela said as she placed another plate of toast on the kitchen table. Perry, Barnaby and Baretta had joined them for breakfast, and now it was only a matter of a few hours before the helicopter would arrive.

"The only thing," she said as she joined the men at the table and picked up her glass of juice, "is that I don't see where the pilot is going to be able to land. There's hardly a clearing big enough for a helicopter that size."

All four men glanced at each other, then looked away.

"What?"

No answer.

She looked at Cameron, and his expression was resigned.

"Now look, Mike, you can't possibly hike all the way back down—"

"You're right. I'll live up here for the rest of my life, do the trial via videotape and even give birth in the jungle and bite the umbilical cord with my own teeth before I'll cross that bridge again."

"I understand your point. But the thing is, Ernie—"

"Ernie?"

"One of the triplets," Baretta cut in. "Rob, Chip and Ernie. Don't worry, *señora*, he's an excellent pilot."

"Where is he landing this helicopter?"

The men looked at each other again, then Cameron sighed and raked his fingers through his hair.

"Well, Mike, it's like this. He's not exactly landing it."

THE HELICOPTER hovered in the sky almost a hundred feet in the air above the thick jungle foliage. Ernie, the pilot, had apparently seen the flare that Cameron had carefully set off near the house.

"This," Michaela said, eyeing Cameron with fury in her eyes, "is almost enough to induce early labor."

"Mike, I'll be right behind you, every step of the way."

"With that gun."

He couldn't seem to help the smile that formed on his mouth. "I learned my lesson the last time. You'll go ahead of any firearms from now on."

"Couldn't we do this later? I mean, why do we have to rush things? Could he come back in an hour or so?"

"Nope. Not a chance. Perry was listening to the radio last night, and there's a chance of a storm front moving in by late afternoon. I want to be off the island in plenty of time to avoid it."

He felt his smile fade as he saw the look on her face and realized what he'd said, remembering their little chat about her various phobias after they'd crossed the bridge.

I'm not crazy about thunderstorms. Lightning and that sort of thing.

"Now, Mike—"

"Cameron, you really know how to ruin a girl's day." She eyed the helicopter, hovering in the clear blue sky, with trepidation. The pilot's assistant was starting to lower a decidedly fragile-looking ladder that swayed in the strong wind much like the bridge from hell.

"Just stick the muzzle of that gun in my back and let's get going."

THUNDER RUMBLED.

Lightning flashed.

Rain drummed an angry tattoo against the helicopter.

Michaela clutched at Cameron's hands, squeezing so hard she feared she'd draw blood. Obviously, Perry was wrong. They hadn't beaten the storm; they'd flown right into it.

As she fretted, Cameron tried to soothe her. Ernie seemed oblivious of the danger. Though his hands were on the controls, his attention was in the back of the plane with his brothers. He was filling them in on their littlest sister's latest escapade.

"So why did Lucy agree to go out on the boat with him in the middle of the night in the first place?" Perry demanded. He was a typical older brother, and something of a know-it-all.

"Hey," said Ernie, clearly an easygoing middle child. "She thought if she could get herself ruined—" he glanced over at Michaela "—you know, compromised, then she could spend the rest of her life with Marco."

Michaela stiffened. Her eyes flicked over to Cameron, but he sat stoically, expressionless.

"What did Papa say?" asked Baretta. He was obviously close to his sister Lucy, and clearly concerned.

"He said," said Ernie, obviously enjoying telling this particular tale, "that being ruined for one night and ruining the rest of your life were two different stories. He's asked Elly Mae to talk some sense into her."

Great. Not only am I stuck in a thunderstorm at a couple of thousand feet with refugees from "My

Three Sons," now I've got to listen to a lecture on ruining my life.

Unwillingly, images of Cameron's lovemaking came back to her. It may have been pitch-black in that hotel suite, but suddenly his face, awash with passion, was clearly visible to her. She saw his intense eyes, his glistening chest. Heard his deep moan at his release. Felt her own again.

At the mere memory, her pale cheeks suffused with color. She wrenched her hands from Cameron's and covered them before he could see. Before any of the brothers could tell she and Lucy had something in common.

Am I ruining the rest of my life, too, trying to make things work with Cameron?

But surely their night together at the Four Seasons Clift was not ruined. No. As she looked over at Cameron, she knew, better than she knew anything else, that she'd never have given up that night of passion. Not for anything in the world.

The brothers gossiped on, oblivious to the rain that lashed down in torrents, the lightning that crackled across the sky.

There was nothing like a tropical storm.

"Sorry about the weather report," Perry called back to Cameron and Michaela. "They said late afternoon, but the guy must have gotten it wrong."

"No problem," said Cameron.

Sure, no problem for you.

He sat there calmly, his head clear, paying no attention to the conversation going on around him. She sat there trying to forget their past, trying to remember how to breathe. Once again, her fingernails were digging into his upper arm, her hands locked around the solid muscle.

She took consolation in one small fact.

If this tin can with rotary blades went down in a blazing ball of fire in the middle of this monsoon, Mr. Control was going with her.

THEY BARELY beat the worst of the storm back to the main house.

Rain was falling in sheets when they arrived, and Ernie did a masterful job of landing the powerful machine on the helipad near the house.

Once inside, Cameron attempted to comfort her.

"It'll be over soon. We can wait it out and fly back tomorrow morning—"

Thunder crashed again, drowning out the rest of his words. In a mere second, lightning lit up the room. Outside, the palm trees were bent almost sideways in the tropical wind.

"Look at it this way," he whispered in her ear, his arms around her. "You've faced almost every single one of your fears on this trip. Not many people can make a claim like that."

"Oh, you think this whole thing has been so funny—"

Her perception shocked him.

"No, I don't. I don't think it's been funny at all."

She looked up at him, and he could tell that being close to him was having a calming effect on her.

"I tell you what," he whispered. "How about if I attempt to distract you and get you through the storm?"

"And what form might this distraction take?"

"Oh, it would be something I'd have to work very hard at."

"Hmm. I like the sound of that."

He led her into the master bedroom, closed the door, and for the remainder of the storm tried to show her, without words, how much he loved her.

EARLY the next morning, the island looked bright and clean, rain-washed, as they drove out to the small airport.

Ernie was there, readying a plane to fly a group of tourists to a deserted island for a picnic.

"Hey, my Papa told me to give you this to take to Julian, with his best regards."

He handed Cameron a bottle of the island's finest golden rum, and Cameron thanked him.

"And Baretta asked me to give this to your wife."

Your wife.

She still started when she heard those words.

Ernie handed her a small box. Coming from Baretta, the box intimidated her.

"It's not alive, is it?" she asked Ernie, eyeing the package with trepidation.

"No. Just my brother's way of saying that you were an awfully good sport."

She opened the box and found a tiny gold pin—of a frog.

"Poisonous, no doubt," she muttered.

Ernie laughed, then waved goodbye and went on his way.

Cameron grinned down at her as she pinned the tiny frog on the lapel of her jacket.

"Be glad it wasn't a frog on a bridge."

The look she gave him spoke volumes.

JULIAN WAS in better spirits—and health—when they reached his side.

"When are you getting me out of here?" he demanded.

"Well, chief, at least now we know he's getting better," Mrs. Monahan remarked, writing something down on her legal pad.

"You're staying right here where the doctors can keep an eye on you until the day of the trial."

Julian didn't look too happy with this, and decided to change the subject.

"When are you getting married?" he asked.

"Right after the trial," Cameron answered, without missing a beat.

Julian didn't miss the startled look Michaela threw Cameron's way.

"Catch him before he changes his stubborn mind," the old man advised. He directed his attention back to Cameron. "Did you bring back Mary's journals like Mrs. Monahan asked you to?"

"We did."

He smiled at Michaela. "I want you to have them, as part of my wedding present to you."

"Oh, but I couldn't..."

"Nonsense. You're family now, and I have a feeling that Mary would want you to have them."

She felt totally overwhelmed by the generosity of his gift, and for a moment simply couldn't reply.

"Thank you, Julian. I'll treasure them."

THERE WAS ANOTHER week left before the trial, and she spent it preparing. Each day she worked on her case, much harder than she would have normally, for she hadn't been in a courtroom for a long time.

Cameron came by every evening after work and took her out to dinner. Both of them avoided discussing the field day the various tabloid papers were having at Julian's expense.

They concentrated on each other.

"What did Dr. Mallory say?" he asked that evening. She'd been to her doctor for her monthly checkup, and found that she liked the fact that Cameron was so deeply involved in her pregnancy.

"He said that I was remarkably fit for a woman who had survived a tropical monsoon, the bridge from hell, and various assorted poisonous flora and fauna."

He started to laugh.

"No, seriously, Mike."

"He said I was fine. Healthy as the proverbial horse. But I have to start thinking about a Lamaze class."

"Would you mind if I... attended the classes with you?"

She waggled a breadstick at him before breaking it in two. "I thought you'd never ask."

THE DAYS PASSED quickly, and before she knew it she was sitting at her desk the night before the trial. She'd gone over her notes until she was in danger of going stale.

Needing to distract herself, she finally gave in to temptation and opened one of Mary's journals.

Later, she thanked the fates profusely. Not only had they had a hand in getting her together with Cameron, they had given her two more gifts. The key to Cameron's heart.

And the evidence she needed to blow Coleman, Watts and Burrell out of the water.

Chapter Eleven

The trial began amid a blaze of publicity.

Michaela was almost blinded by flashbulbs as she stepped out of the low, sleek limousine that pulled up to the courthouse steps. Cameron was right behind her the entire way, watching out for her. But he couldn't field the questions.

"Do you really think Julian Black stole the logo from that poor woman?"

"How has he gotten away with fooling us for so many years?"

"How could he have done that to a helpless, eight-year-old girl? She was only trying to win a contest and help her family!"

Joshua Burrell's media connections had been working overtime. Michaela hated reading the papers, seeing what they were doing to Julian's good name with sly innuendo and speculation, but she had to be prepared for the public's perception of this particular case.

It was going to be tough finding an impartial jury.

Once inside, she realized that even in the courtroom they weren't to be spared from the sight of various reporters. She approached the front, Cameron by her side, and nodded coolly to Carl Rowling, one of Burrell's yes-men.

A good lawyer, but a man utterly content to let someone else make all his decisions for him.

The judge was a woman she'd heard of, and respected. Diane Cole. She was older, and had a stern, but fair manner of working. Michaela set her briefcase on her table and unsnapped it, then began arranging various papers and articles. Once she was satisfied that she had everything she needed at hand, she set her briefcase on the floor next to her chair, and quietly sat down.

The hoopla was deafening, and only rose when Julian was escorted into the courtroom, Mrs. Monahan at his side. He looked tired. Michaela could see he was exerting considerable strength of will. Only a few days ago he had privately signed the toy company over to Cameron, claiming that whatever the outcome of this trial, he was going to spend the rest of his life doing exactly what he wanted to do. And if that included skipping a couple of days at the office, then that was that.

Julian was a proud man, and it had cost him to let go of his company. But he had wanted to do what was best for everyone involved. Michaela knew the old man wouldn't go down without a fight. She was determined to see that it was a fair one.

She kept all of her senses alert, especially when the woman who had accused Julian of this crucial theft entered the room. Carl, obsequious as always, rose to meet her and escort her to his table.

Michaela glanced at her watch. Within minutes, the first day of the trial would begin.

Cameron came and sat down next to her. As the acting head of Teddy's Toys, he was the one who had formally hired her to defend the firm. Here, in the courtroom, he was completely formal with her, and Michaela was grateful for that professional courtesy.

She was also grateful for the suit she'd chosen for the first day. A charcoal-gray pinstripe, it was beautifully cut. She looked chunky, not pregnant.

Chunky, she could live with.

Unmarried, and pregnant to boot, could be detrimental to the case.

Judge Cole swept into the courtroom, the folds of her black robe billowing around her as she walked. An African-American, she had a regal, queenly air, and Michaela felt a sudden surge of hope.

Surely this woman would see that justice was served.

Then the gavel came down with a resounding crack, and the trial of Sally Riker v. Teddy's Toys began.

THE MORNING was largely spent giving the jury a complete and thorough background of the case. Michaela's strategy was to show Julian and Mary building their business together, the passion of their vision, and how hard they'd worked.

A perfect example of the American Dream.

She pulled out every stop she knew, including injecting her courtroom personality with a considerable amount of warmth. Several of the jury members were older, and she was counting on the fact that they could relate to Julian's lifelong struggle, how hard he and his wife had worked.

The plaintiff's lawyer took a different tactic, emphasizing how much money Julian possessed, how wealthy Teddy's Toys had made him.

Michaela had expected this and retaliated by noting how many millions Julian had consistently given to various charities over the years, especially charities that dealt with animals and children.

It was an exhausting morning, and by the time they broke for lunch, Michaela was feeling the strain.

Cameron ducked outside the courthouse to find a secluded pay phone. Making sure no one was around, he placed his call.

Dr. Mallory wasn't worried.

"She's healthy. She's a strong woman." He laughed. "You know, if she can walk miles through a Caribbean jungle, fighting it out in the courtroom should be the proverbial piece of cake. She loves a good battle, you know that, Cameron."

He sighed. Watching Michaela in court had been a complete revelation. He'd realized he was in for a number of highly stimulating arguments once they were married.

"Is there anything I should watch out for?"

There was a short silence on the other end of the line before Dr. Mallory replied. "The only thing that's worried me about her pregnancy were those two times she fainted. No, I remember it was only once. The other time, she said you helped her sit down, then she felt better. If she starts to feel dizzy, make her take it easy."

"Will do."

THE DAY FINISHED with the jury brought up to date, and tomorrow opening arguments would begin. Michaela felt exhausted, and when she reached the safety and shelter of the corporate limousine, she leaned her head back against the seat and closed her eyes.

"You were brilliant," Cameron said.

His quiet admiration warmed her, and she reached for his hand.

"Thank you for being there for me."

"I didn't even think you knew I was there." She hadn't looked at him once while she'd been making her various arguments.

"I knew. Just having you there was more of a support than you'll ever know."

THE FOLLOWING DAY, the battle began in earnest.

Carl Rowling went after Julian with a subtle viciousness. He painted a picture of a man who, while possessing absolutely no creativity of his own, exploited and manipulated the creative gifts of others to build an empire of wealth.

Michaela retaliated by showing example after example of Julian's generosity toward his employees, even asking a few who had been with the company for more than a decade to take the stand.

Their comments about Julian Black moved the jury emotionally, she could tell.

Then Sally Riker took the stand.

She'd been advised brilliantly by the collective legal mind of Coleman, Watts and Burrell. Even Michaela had to admit that. Outfitted very conservatively, but in a manner that conveyed she didn't have a lot of money. In a subtle print dress, with her soft gray hair pulled back in a bun, she looked like everyone's imaginary grandma.

That meant trouble. The jury would be predisposed to be sympathetic toward her.

But she was also nervous. Too nervous. In fact, she looked frightened.

Michaela had a sudden hunch that someone else was behind this dirty little accusation. Someone who was going to profit if Sally won her lawsuit.

The press had had a field day speculating as to why Julian hadn't simply paid her off out of court. Shut her up with hush money.

Now, as Sally took the stand, Michaela watched her lawyer as he questioned her, and she tried to find a loophole, an inconsistency, anything.

Finally, it was her turn to question the witness.

"Mrs. Riker, have you ever purchased any of the toys that Julian Black manufactures?"

Sally hesitated. But she was under oath.

"I just bought my granddaughter another teddy bear for her birthday. She collects them."

"And would you say that you received quality for your money?"

"Yes. She loves the bear... and the others I've bought her have... lasted."

"So it would be safe to say that you don't consider Teddy's Toys to be a cheap sort of outfit."

She hesitated, then looked to her lawyer as if asking for guidance. But Sally was clearly nearsighted, and had chosen not to wear her glasses on the stand.

She hesitated, flustered.

"Mrs. Riker?" Michaela asked softly.

"Objection! The defense is harassing the witness!" Carl Rowling barked, jumping up from his seat.

"I'd hardly call that harassment," Judge Cole said dryly. She turned to Michaela. "You may continue."

"Mrs. Riker?"

"They are excellent toys," Sally Riker said softly, and Michaela sensed that the woman was quietly miserable.

She changed her line of questioning.

"How many children do you have, Mrs. Riker?"

"Five."

"And grandchildren?"

She hesitated again, clearly upset by the question.

"Seven."

Michaela smiled at the woman, trying to capture that elusive feeling of trust. "What sorts of toys did you buy your children when they were little?"

Sally Riker flushed, then admitted, "The bears were their favorites."

"Did it hurt you, when you first saw the bear known as Bandit Bear?"

Sally looked puzzled.

"Exhibit A, please."

A medium-size stuffed bear with distinctive facial markings was brought to Michaela, and she placed the toy in Sally's hands.

"Do you recognize this bear as Bandit Bear?"

Sally nodded her head.

Michaela felt a sudden rush of sympathy for the older woman. She didn't belong here, she didn't want to be here, and she felt with overwhelming certainty that the woman was someone else's pawn.

But whose?

"I need you to answer the question with a yes or a no. Mrs. Riker, do you recognize this bear as Bandit Bear?"

"Yes."

"And did you ever give any of your five children one of the bears that Teddy's Toys makes known as Bandit Bear?"

"Y-yes."

"Did you feel a sense of anger?"

"What do you mean?"

"When you recognized the design as your own?"

Teddy Bear Heir

"Objection, Your Honor!" Carl Rowling called. "The defense is leading the witness."

"Objection overruled," Judge Cole said evenly. "Please continue."

"Did you feel a sense of anger or loss when you recognized the design as your own?"

"No, not then... later."

"And that was why you chose to bring this matter to court, some fifty years later?"

Sally Riker seemed confused.

"Mrs. Riker? What made you decide to finally bring this matter before a court of law?"

"I needed... I thought that I... I didn't think that Julian Black should be the only one to... profit through my design."

"Thank you, Mrs. Riker, I have no other questions for you at this time."

They broke for lunch.

"SOMETHING DOESN'T smell right about this," Michaela said as she finished up lunch with Cameron and Julian. Cameron was peeling an orange and handing her sections of the citrus fruit, while Julian barely ate a thing.

"I was thinking the same thoughts myself," Julian mused. "She looks scared to death up on the stand."

"I'm going to call Chuck," Cameron said, referring to his writer friend who was also something of a private detective when he wanted to be. But more importantly, he knew a few genuinely good ones.

MICHAELA HAD BEEN dreading the moment when Julian would be brought to the stand, but he was called as a witness right after lunch.

Rowling was unmerciful as he grilled him, and Michaela stepped in as many times as she dared. Julian had told her privately, before the trial, to "let that young whippersnapper have his way with me. That'll show the jury what kind of garbage Coleman, Watts and Burrell are hiring!" But there were several times during the proceedings that Michaela had had to step in.

Finally it was her turn to question him, and she decided to go straight for the evidence.

"Mr. Black, do you recognize this book?"

"Yes."

"What is it?"

"My journal."

"I've marked a certain section. Could I ask you to read it out loud?"

"Certainly."

He did so in a remarkably strong, clear voice.

The section he read dealt with the night he and Mary had created the little bear known the world over as Bandit Bear.

Michaela listened as Julian read. He and Mary had been poor at the time, but one of their favorite pastimes had been to go to the Bay City Zoo on Tuesday afternoons when admission was free. On one particular outing they learned that several animals had recently been rescued from a shabby circus and been given sanctuary at the zoo. As Julian particularly liked bears, he'd been glad to hear that two little brown bear cubs had been rescued.

He and Mary had stood looking at the bears, but only one had come out. Later they had talked to one of the zoo personnel.

"The other one won't come out," he'd told them. "Pretty badly abused. Just sits in the corner of the cave we made for 'em."

Julian, as poor as they had been, had determined to contribute to the zoo's protection program from that moment on, for, as he'd written in his journal, both animals and children were the silent sufferers of society, and had no voice to give to the injustices done to them.

Michaela knew she'd picked the right passage for him to read, as the courtroom had grown suddenly silent.

"Why did you think up the contest, Mr. Black, almost a full year later?"

"I wanted some children to have fun, and I donated every cent of the entry fees to the Bay City Zoo."

"And did you ever see this entry?" She held up the scrap of colored paper that constituted Exhibit B, Sally Riker's contest entry.

"I never did. The contest was judged by a panel of employees. I wanted them to have a little fun, as well, feel like they were really part of the company. I don't recall that particular entry making it into the final rounds."

"It did not. Thank you, Mr. Black. Oh, just one more question."

"Certainly."

"Whatever happened to that bear cub?"

"Well," said Julian, obviously enjoying the memory. "That bear's handler, his name was Bob. And that man worked with that bear until he could trust again and was no longer afraid to come outside. The day that animal walked out into the sunlight, Bob gave me a telephone call, and Mary and I rushed right down there. I saw that little face, and all that hard-earned character, and I said, 'Mary, that's our bear!' And Bandit Bear was born."

"And that period is also recorded in your journal, Mr. Black?"

"Yes, it is. Would you like me to read it?"

She smiled at him. Julian was getting some of his fighting spirit back.

"No, that won't be necessary. I believe you."

"And I do, as well, Mr. Black."

Michaela looked up at Judge Cole. The woman's dark brown eyes were shining as she leaned forward.

"My mother took me to see that bear when I was a very little girl, and I never forgot the look in that animal's eyes."

Carl Rowling was visibly sweating.

"He was an inspiration to me," Julian said quietly.

Judge Cole nodded. She glanced at Carl Rowling.

"Do you wish to question the witness further?"
"No, Your Honor."

THE JURY voted in Julian's favor, and his name was cleared.

Chuck and his P.I. friend found out that Sally Riker had a rather unscrupulous older brother who had seen a chance to make a fast buck. Sally had only complied because she had a young grandson who was seriously ill, and her brother had promised her a share if she went along with his scheme.

Julian offered to put her in touch with one of his charities that offered medical care to families that could not afford it. He assured her he would personally make sure her little grandson got the treatment he needed.

And Michaela received more publicity and job offers than she'd ever had in her life.

A few days after the trial, Cameron had dinner with Michaela at the restaurant where they had once talked about the original marital contract. And he wondered if now was the time to tell her there would never be a contract between them.

What he felt for her ran too deep for a legal document.

She was in his heart, his mind, his blood to a degree that there was no more choice involved. It wasn't a matter of whether he was scared of love or not. He had to be with her. He had to help her, protect her, see her through the birth of their child.

And once that child was born, he would care for both of them, put his very life on the line if necessary.

He'd learned another lesson on Julian's infernal quest. Love didn't give you any choices. Love was all there was in the end.

He leaned toward Michaela, giving her his complete attention, then frowned as he noticed someone approaching their table. Since the trial, Michaela had become something of a celebrity, and now he was sure someone else was about to offer her yet another job.

He'd guessed right.

She looked at him for guidance, but he loved her enough that he knew she'd been badly hurt by what Joshua Burrell had done to her, professionally. Now, it was sweet revenge on the firm of Coleman, Watts and Burrell for her to be able to have her pick of any law firm in the city. And for Joshua Burrell to know it, and realize what he had lost.

He sat back and let her be a star.

And loved her.

"GO TO SLEEP," he said, smoothing the hair off her forehead and kissing her. She looked like the most lovely of princesses, all tucked into her beautiful brass bed, her dark auburn hair fanned out over the lacy pillowcase.

Her bedroom had been a revelation. For as much as his Michaela was a tough, no-nonsense lawyer during the day, her bedroom revealed a softer side of her personality.

"But we didn't have much time to talk—"

He kissed her again. "You were yawning over dessert." He smiled down at her. "It's okay—"

Michaela.

He thought of saying her name, of bringing her that little bit closer. Then he saw the shadows beneath her eyes.

His Michaela was a fighter, but this last fight had taken a lot more out of her than he'd thought.

"It's okay, Mike. We have all the time in the world."

"Do we?"

He saw the worried look in her eyes.

"I promise."

She smiled, then snuggled deeper beneath the covers.

"You're so good to me, Cameron."

You're so good to me, Cameron.

He thought about what she'd said later that night, sitting in the nursery, and realized he hadn't been good to her at all. Keeping her at arm's length. Fighting for control.

Control of what? Once you lost your heart, there was no longer any control.

Control? If one accepted the fact that life was basically chaotic, that things happened in the most random of manners, then all you could do was hope for the love that would get you through those darkest nights.

He thought of Julian, alone. Dirty and scruffy, sitting on that balcony. Of the look in his eyes when he'd turned to face him.

He thought of Mary, his grandmother, and the sounds of her sobbing, the quietly choked sound that had floated across the hallway into his bedroom. She'd lost her only son the same night he'd lost his father, and he'd loved his grandmother so much he'd hurt with her.

He thought of Michaela, losing her father, and wondered how she'd found the strength to go on.

Cameron sat in the rocking chair by the window, looking out over the garden. He couldn't see much of it in the dark, but he'd spent enough time gazing out this nursery window that he knew where everything was. He thought of his child, coming into the world and growing up in this house. Knowing Mike Larkin through the home he'd created, the things he'd loved.

His eyes burned.

It hurt to remember, but he had to go back. Just this once. He had to go back and remember what had happened, the slow steps, the many little choices he'd made that had set him on the dangerous path to not caring. Not feeling.

Not loving.

There were many things he claimed he couldn't remember. Julian would laugh over a particular memory, and Cameron would smile and pretend. But he'd blocked a lot out.

He'd never been able to forget the night his parents had died.

The current nanny had been down in the kitchen, arguing with the cook. He'd been in the nursery, and had turned on the television at the far end of the great room.

The smoking plane had captured his attention instantly.

The picture of his mother and father had confused him at first, but he'd been a bright little boy. Slowly, listening to the newscaster, he'd realized what had happened.

And blamed himself.

He hadn't wanted them to go, he'd never wanted them to go, but for whatever reason, they hadn't wanted to spend a great deal of time at home. Before they'd left the last time, he'd thrown a temper tantrum to end them all, and been sent to bed with no supper.

His mother had come to kiss him goodbye, and he'd smelled her expensive perfume in the darkened nursery. As furiously hurt as only a young child can be, he'd turned his head so her lavishly glossed lips could only graze the top of his head.

"I'll bring you back a present, Cam," she'd whispered, and then she was gone.

And then she was gone forever.

He'd left the television on the night of the crash, and hidden in one of the long, deep closets in his parents' bedroom. He'd barely heard the screams coming from the kitchen. He'd heard nothing, until Mary Black found him hiding, one of his mother's shoes in his arms, one of her sweaters over his shoulders.

If he could still smell her, then she couldn't be gone. For as much as she had not really warmed up to motherhood, he'd loved her with the passionate love of a child. He'd never stopped loving her, and he'd sent her on her way without even giving her a kiss.

Mary had gathered him up into her arms, but even then he'd stiffened, pulled away from her, gone deep inside himself where he would never hurt anyone, or be hurt again.

It was a strange thing, which memories were the most vivid. He'd never forget the tone in her voice as she'd called to him, then the look on her face when she finally found him. His grandmother had understood children, and he knew with the simplicity of a child's wisdom that if it hadn't been for her perseverance, he probably would have died.

A part of him had.

His eyes burned fiercely, and tears he'd held inside for decades finally began to fall. And he knew, from one of the carefully picked books his grandmother had read to him, that the Tin Man had been right. He finally knew he had a heart, for that heart was breaking.

He sat back in the rocking chair and let the tears fall, let the emotion take him until he was exhausted from it. Then, wiping his eyes, he glanced around the nursery.

Teddy Bear Heir

If there was one room that exemplified hope, it was a child's nursery. Children represented hope, and Julian had known this when he'd sent him on his so-called quest in the first place.

Children represented light and hope and warmth, the best anyone could give the world.

Moving stiffly, still filled with emotion, Cameron picked up the stuffed bear he'd set on the floor and looked at the quizzical little face. Bandit Bear. A logo known throughout the world. An empire.

All because of a damaged little bear who hadn't wanted to come out of his cave.

Cameron smiled tiredly.

And a damaged little boy who'd wanted to stay hidden forever, tucked away in his parents' closet. Until Mary had chosen to take him into her arms and away from all the pain.

He was surprised by the effort just that one smile took. Even the bear had the sense to finally come out of its cave and try...

His eyes filled again as he realized he'd always had people around him who had loved him. Yet he'd stayed hidden.

Julian and Mary had done their best by him, and tried to let him see the world wasn't always a cruel and terrible place.

And Michaela had blazed into his life and refused to settle for anything but the best.

His love.

He thought of her as he set the stuffed bear on the floor, then tilted his head back so it rested against the smooth wood of the rocking chair.

And he thought of the future for the first time, without fear.

About the child he wanted to help bring into the world, and all the dangers that world held in store for him.

And all the joy, Michaela would stubbornly insist.

He smiled through his tears as he realized who she'd reminded him of from the start. Mary. Both women continually turned toward the light, while he and his grandfather had a tendency to remain in the dark.

Not anymore.

He wouldn't be able to tell her all of it. Not yet. If he could get through asking her to marry him, letting her know he loved her with all his heart, then take her safely through the birth of their child, he would be able to find the words to tell her that she had given him a gift beyond any he'd ever received.

For in her stubborn refusal to settle for anything but his love, Michaela had given him back a crucial piece of his soul.

THEY RETURNED to the island a week later for Julian's infamous Fourth of July victory party. He gave a bash every Independence Day, filling the house—or mansion, as Michaela still chose to think of it—to overflowing with friends and family. But this year, it was especially celebratory, what with Teddy's Toys' courtroom triumph. It was a full-scale blowout, black tie with a formal sit-down dinner for the scores of guests Julian had invited.

"I just hope he doesn't ask Manny to sing a few tunes," Michaela said as she and Cameron walked into the elegant party.

"I don't think he will, but I do know that the whole family's invited."

"Really!"

"They're celebrating, as well," he said. "Perry's wife just had her first child."

"Don't tell me. They named it Gilligan."

"No. Twins. Maddie and David."

THE PARTY SPARKLED; everyone commented about how excellent the dinner was, how wonderful the music from the steel band sounded, how fabulous Julian looked. And he did look good. Julian Theodore Black had put his trial behind him and now looked forward to the good times.

Cameron caught sight of his grandfather by the champagne.

"Having a good time?" he asked him.

"I'd have a better time if you'd hurry up and marry that girl before she gets away."

"Grandfather—"

Julian held up a hand to still any protests. "I'm sorry, Cameron. These things need to be said. I should have had this talk with you long ago."

Without preamble, he charged headlong into a litany of questions. "When are you going to wake up and see how much she's got to offer you? And I don't just mean the baby. When are you going to realize you two need each other? What's it going to take to make you fall in love with her? Why can't you—"

"I already am."

"If you'd just take a good look at your life and realize that running the world's biggest toy company doesn't amount to a hill of beans— What did you say?"

"I love her."

Julian looked stunned. "When did you come to this realization?"

"In the last week or so."

"And you haven't told her!"

"Things have been pretty hectic. I've been waiting for the right time. A peaceful moment, just the two of us. You've got to admit, Jules, they've been in short supply."

While he talked, a smile had broken out on his grandfather's face. He'd never seen the man look so utterly happy.

"That they have, my boy. That they have." His blue eyes twinkled shrewdly. "So, if you had to take this particular quest all over again, what do you think you'd learn?"

"That love's the only thing worth fighting for. The only thing there is, when you come right down to it."

Teddy Bear Heir 237

He was enveloped in a fierce bear hug by Julian, and the emotion in that quick, physical gesture almost overwhelmed him.

Julian stepped back, not mindful of the tears forming in his eyes.

"So the prince wins the prize, after all," he whispered. He touched his grandson's cheek with a shaky hand.

"Oh, Cameron, Mary would be so proud of you."

The party went on into the wee hours of the morning, but Michaela was enjoying herself immensely. She'd taken a long nap earlier in the afternoon, for she'd planned to party all night. Now, thinking about tasting yet another one of the culinary delights that Julian had provided for his guests, she saw him gesture her over.

Grabbing an enormous strawberry that had been dipped in white chocolate, she headed his way.

"I don't think I told you, young lady, what an outstanding job I thought you did in that courtroom."

"Oh, only about a couple of dozen times a day for the last week."

Julian's blue eyes twinkled. "Where's that young man of yours?"

"He went to get something to drink. He'll be back shortly."

"Try to manage a moment alone with him, if you can."

"Why, Julian, do you know something that I don't?"

"Maybe, maybe."

He looked so delighted that she couldn't help smiling back.

"Your father would have been proud of you in that courtroom. I wish Mike could have seen you."

Her smile faded just a little on the inside as memories took hold of her. She'd felt so very bittersweet the morning after the trial, reading the papers in the sunny living room of her Victorian home. Mike Larkin would have loved the various articles about her, would have laughed out loud as he'd read them, would have bought multiple copies of the paper, sent copies to distant relatives, and put several of the best up on the refrigerator.

She'd put her favorite up with a funny little magnet of a lobster he'd bought her down at Fisherman's Wharf one afternoon. She'd looked at it, the newsprint contrasting against the cool white appliance, but the feeling hadn't been the same.

She needed someone to love her the way Mike Larkin had loved her. Unconditionally. Totally. Forever.

"Michaela? Did I say something wrong?"

"No. No, Julian." She touched his arm, reassuring him, knowing that if she didn't get away soon, she was going to burst into tears.

"Michaela, if I—"

"I'm going to take a walk on the beach. I think I need a little time by myself." Handing him the uneaten strawberry, she turned and walked swiftly out of the room.

THE BEACH was empty, which was fine by her. There were a series of paths that cut through the terraced garden to a long flight of stone steps that led to the sand. She took off her sandals at the foot of the steps and left them there, then started walking along the water's edge.

Dawn would be coming soon, and with it some tough decisions.

She'd never signed that contract she'd drawn up for Cameron's wife-to-be. He'd asked her to, that day in the nursery. But then, on the island, it seemed as if things had changed. As if he had changed. And then Julian fell ill and the trial had consumed them.

The time had come to figure out what would happen to them for the rest of their lives.

Her hands splayed over her belly; she instinctively rubbed the baby they'd created. She needed to figure out what would happen to them when the baby came.

What would happen after her baby was born? Then Cameron would have the heir he'd set out to find five months ago. Would it change the way he felt about her?

She wondered what kind of a father he'd be. And if she'd even be around to judge.

Tears welled in her eyes. It hurt so very badly to know Cameron would never be capable of loving her the way she loved him.

The baby will love you...

She looked out across the moonlight on the water.

The baby would be a comfort to her. Such a miracle, how they loved you so totally, with every bit of strength in their tiny hearts.

What happened to cause people to close up, to be incapable of love?

The time she'd spent out in the world had made her realize what a truly extraordinary man her father had been. For fate had dealt Mike Larkin a hand that would have made most men incredibly bitter. Yet he'd still had so much to give his daughter, his community, his world.

"You were right about Cameron," she whispered, remembering the words her father had said after meeting him. Something about making sure that he loved you, or else...

Or else it would be what I have now.

"I followed my heart, Pop. I just didn't think it would turn out this badly. Oh, I don't mean *that* badly. I'm going to be a mother, and I never thought that would happen. I have my health, I have work that I love..."

The star that she'd always thought of as his winked furiously in the night sky, and she could almost hear his rich, deep voice.

Not enough, my girl. Not enough...

"Oh, I know." She paused to collect her thoughts.

"Why is it," she began, her voice tight, "that I can fight a court case to the very end, hike across a jungle and even walk across a bridge hundreds of feet up in the air, and I can't seem to figure out how to make him love me?"

She could almost hear her father's laughter. Certainly not malicious, simply full of love for her and the ironies of life. And the memory made her smile.

"Funny, huh? I was so sure that all it would be was that one night. And I could have lived with that, 'cause I'm like you, Pop. I make my decisions and I stand by them."

She walked a little closer to the water, letting the foaming waves curl over her feet.

"Who am I trying to fool? It wasn't just one night." She placed a hand on the curve of her abdomen again. "Even if there hadn't been a baby, even if there had never been a baby, it would have been forever. For me. After that night."

The star twinkled in the sky and it comforted her to think that, somehow, her father just might be listening.

"So what do I do, Pop? What am I going to do?"

She thought of her father, and then of Mary, whose voice had spoken to her from within the pages of her journals. And it was within those journals that she'd learned that Julian's and Mary's marriage had not been easy, that they had had their share of troubles and arguments. And one of the major ones had been that Julian had struggled against his heart and what it had tried to tell him from the moment he'd met Mary.

Words from the journal flitted into her mind.

Oh, I know that stubborn fool. After I'm gone, he'll tell everyone that it was some nonsense like love at first sight. Well maybe it was, but that still didn't make it easy for my Jules. Why is it that women believe love adds to their lives, while to a certain kind of man, it is a weakness, and to be avoided?

Like grandfather, like grandson. They were so alike, and couldn't see it. Stubborn, proud, and sometimes even afraid.

With a baby on the way, she didn't have the luxury of making certain types of choices. Now every choice for the rest of her life had to be the best choice for her child.

"Then I'll stay with him," she whispered into the sky.

She could almost feel her father's love and approval, surrounding her, embracing her.

"Because sometimes," she said, repeating words she'd heard him tell her over and over again, "we have to make choices in this life that aren't always about us."

He'd taught her well.

She tried to find the star again. Dawn was breaking, and it was fading into the lilacs, pinks and golds of the morning sky.

"Thanks, Pop," she whispered, looking out over the horizon. "You'll never know how much."

She'd never had the chance to truly thank him, and now all she wanted to tell him was that she hoped she could be half the parent to her unborn child that he had been to her.

She walked over to the base of a huge palm tree. Sitting down on the cool sand, heedless of her evening dress, she surrendered to her emotions and finally cried.

HE'D FOLLOWED HER to the beach, but when he'd started to approach her, sensed she was involved in thoughts and feelings so private that he shouldn't disturb them.

He watched her cry, and knew he was the cause.

When she got up and started to walk slowly along the beach, he went after her.

And he knew, in his heart, that he'd never find a better time than now.

"MICHAELA!"

She turned at the sound of her name and saw him. He was walking toward her on the beach, in his tuxedo pants and shirt, but had discarded his jacket and his shoes. Barefoot, he looked beautiful and proud, like a pirate king in his own little kingdom.

She wiped her cheeks and hoped he couldn't tell she'd been crying.

She mustered a smile, but knew it didn't reach her eyes.

"Michaela."

Something was wrong.

Michaela... not Mike.

Her heart started to pick up speed.

He took both her hands in his, and tightly held on to them, as if they were a sort of lifeline. And all of a sudden, she knew they were.

She didn't say a word, as anticipation so thick and sweet crowded her throat. Her heart was pounding so furiously she could barely hear the sound of the waves around their feet. The bottoms of his tuxedo pants were getting wet, and he didn't even notice.

He simply touched her hair, her face, then kissed her forehead, looked into her eyes...

"Michaela, I love you."

She started to tremble inside as she realized that every dream she'd ever wanted was about to come true, on this beach, at this moment. The only thing she'd ever wanted in her life was Cameron's love, and he was finally giving it to her.

She must not have moved at all because he said it again, this time dropping to his knees in front of her in the wet sand, putting his arms around her, and ruining those beautiful pants once and for all.

"I love you and I can't live without you. I need you, Michaela, to make me laugh, to argue, to help me raise our child, to share a life that I promise you will be as good as I can possibly make it."

Her hands moved to his hair in a daze, then she pressed the side of his head against her rounded stomach, holding him against her until her legs started trembling so badly she could barely stand.

He stood, swung her up into his arms and carried her to the shelter of the palm trees, where he sat down and cradled her in his lap.

"Say my name," she whispered, her face buried in his neck as tears streamed down her face.

"Michaela. Oh, darling, don't cry."

"Say it again, and don't ever call me Mike again."

"Michaela, I love you. Only you." He kissed the top of her head and held her tightly against him.

"Forever."

MARY FIONA Larkin Black was born almost three weeks past her due date, at exactly four minutes after midnight on a damp and foggy December Twenty-fifth.

Christmas Day. A day for miracles.

"Well, Julius," said Mrs. Monahan, "according to my calculations, she has a third house sun in Capricorn, her moon is in the twelfth house, and she has Libra rising." She pushed back the cap of her elf costume and gave the top of her head a scratch.

Julian, dressed as Santa Claus and making his yearly tour of the children's ward in one of his favorite San Francisco hospitals, couldn't take his eyes off the soundly sleeping infant in the nursery.

His great-granddaughter was absolutely perfect.

"And what does all that mean?"

"That she'll be beautiful—"

"Of course she is. Look at her."

"That, hopefully, she'll have a few siblings to interact with."

"Michaela will see to that. After what Cameron saw her go through, he's already decided there will be no more babies."

Mrs. Monahan stifled a decidedly unelflike laugh.

"She'll possess a strong will, and be quite a handful."

"As have all the Blacks, since time immemorial. And it will serve my grandson right."

Mrs. Monahan sighed as she looked at the peacefully sleeping infant. "And she's an old soul. That twelfth house moon does it every time."

"Just what they need, Mrs. M. And isn't it amazing how the universe always seems to give us exactly what we need—if we're smart enough to ask for it."

"It is, indeed."

HE COULDN'T believe she was smiling at him after all the pain she'd endured.

"So, you'll still sleep in the same bed with me?" he said, his tone light. He hoped she wouldn't realize that he was only partly joking.

"Please. I've crossed the bridge to the heavens, or whatever that thing was called. Labor and delivery were a snap compared to that."

"It didn't look like a snap."

"I'd have three or four more before I'd even look at that gorge again." Her eyes brightened and she sat up in bed as the night nurse carried the newest addition to the Black family into the private room, Julian and Mrs. Monahan at her heels.

"Now what have you been up to?" she teased her grandfather-in-law.

"He's only promised every single child who's being admitted to surgery a huge teddy bear and any sundae they want at Ghiradelli Square," Mrs. Monahan said, looking at Julian fondly and shaking her head.

"That's a lot of ice cream," Cameron remarked.

"No, my boy, that is a lot of hope." Julian's eyes softened as he gazed at his great-granddaughter. "I do believe she has Mike's eyes. And Mary's nose."

"How fortunate it wasn't the other way around," Cameron remarked, and Michaela laughed.

After Mary Fiona had nursed her fill and gone back to the nursery, Mrs. Monahan gave Julian a gentle pinch in the ribs.

"Weren't you going to take me to that new Southern restaurant everyone's raving about so we can celebrate this event properly?"

"Sapphire's Place. Of course, of course. Nancy promised they'd keep the kitchen open for us, no matter how late we arrived." Julian took the hint quickly, and gave Cameron a quick pat on the shoulder. "We'll leave you two alone."

They were gone within minutes, leaving him alone with his wife. She lay quietly in bed, her eyes closed, and for a moment he thought she'd fallen asleep.

"Would you do it again?" she whispered, and he smiled, then leaned over, brushed the hair off her forehead and kissed her gently. She looked so tired, and deserved a little rest.

"Would you?" he asked softly. She opened one eye and he smiled down at her. "After all, you were the one who made the first move."

She opened her other eye and sat up a little in bed.

"I did, didn't I?" She sounded so pleased with herself. "And I would. I would do anything, anything at all, to arrive at this place with you." Tears glinted in her eyes.

"Thank you for giving me a daughter, Cameron Black."

He could barely speak, he was so overcome with emotion. Then he found his voice and knew the one thing he had to say, the thing he had to let her know.

"Thank you for giving me back to myself, Michaela."

"Oh, Cameron," she whispered just before he kissed her.

HARLEQUIN®

Weddings, Inc.

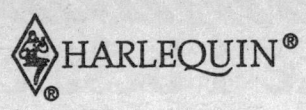

Harlequin Books requests the pleasure of your company this June in Eternity, Massachusetts, for WEDDINGS, INC.

For generations, couples have been coming to Eternity, Massachusetts, to exchange wedding vows. Legend has it that those married in Eternity's chapel are destined for a lifetime of happiness. And the residents are more than willing to give the legend a hand.

Beginning in June, you can experience the legend of Eternity. Watch for one title per month, across all of the Harlequin series.

HARLEQUIN BOOKS... NOT THE SAME OLD STORY!

WEDGEN

Take 4 bestselling love stories FREE

Plus get a FREE surprise gift!

Special Limited-time Offer

Mail to Harlequin Reader Service®

    3010 Walden Avenue
    P.O. Box 1867
    Buffalo, N.Y. 14269-1867

YES! Please send me 4 free Harlequin American Romance® novels and my free surprise gift. Then send me 4 brand-new novels every month, which I will receive months before they appear in bookstores. Bill me at the low price of $2.89 each plus 25¢ delivery and applicable sales tax, if any.* That's the complete price and—compared to the cover prices of $3.50 each—quite a bargain! I understand that accepting the books and gift places me under no obligation ever to buy any books. I can always return a shipment and cancel at any time. Even if I never buy another book from Harlequin, the 4 free books and the surprise gift are mine to keep forever.

154 BPA ANRL

Name _____ (PLEASE PRINT)

Address _____ Apt. No. _____

City _____ State _____ Zip _____

This offer is limited to one order per household and not valid to present Harlequin American Romance® subscribers. *Terms and prices are subject to change without notice. Sales tax applicable in N.Y.

UAM-94R   ©1990 Harlequin Enterprises Limited

HARLEQUIN AMERICAN ROMANCE

American Romance is goin' to the chapel...with three soon-to-be-wed couples. Only thing is, saying "I do" is the farthest thing from their minds!

You're cordially invited to join us for three months of veils and vows. Don't miss any of the nuptials in

May 1994	#533 THE EIGHT-SECOND WEDDING by Anne McAllister
June 1994	#537 THE KIDNAPPED BRIDE by Charlotte Maclay
July 1994	#541 VEGAS VOWS by Linda Randall Wisdom

GTC

HARLEQUIN SUPERROMANCE®

TIRED OF WINTER?
ESCAPE THE WINTER BLUES THIS SPRING WITH HARLEQUIN SUPERROMANCE AND

MARRIOTT'S

Camelback Inn
RESORT, GOLF CLUB & SPA

Mobil Five Star, AAA Five Diamond Award Winner
5402 East Lincoln Drive, Scottsdale, Arizona 85253, (602) 948-1700

April Showers brings a shower of new authors! Harlequin Superromance is highlighting four simply sensational new authors. Four provocative, passionate, romantic stories guaranteed to put Spring into your heart!

May is the month for flowers, and with flowers comes ROMANCE! Join us in May as four of our most popular authors—Tracy Hughes, Janice Kaiser, Lynn Erickson and Bobby Hutchinson—bring you four of their most romantic Superromance titles.

And to really escape the winter blues, enter our Superromantic Weekend Sweepstakes. You could win an exciting weekend at the Marriott's Camelback Inn, Resort, Golf Club and Spa in Scottsdale, Arizona. Look for further details in all Harlequin Superromance novels.

HARLEQUIN SUPERROMANCE...
NOT THE SAME OLD STORY!

HSREL3

HARLEQUIN AMERICAN ROMANCE

THE BABY IS ADORABLE...
BUT WHICH MAN IS HIS DADDY?

Alec Roman: He found baby Andy in a heart-shaped Valentine basket—but were finders necessarily keepers?

Jack Rourke: During his personal research into Amish culture, he got close to an Amish beauty—so close he thought he was the father.

Grady Noland: The tiny bundle of joy softened this rogue cop—and made him want to own up to what he thought were his responsibilities.

Cathy Gillen Thacker brings you TOO MANY DADS, a three-book series that asks the all-important question: Which man is about to become a daddy?

Too Many DADS

If you missed any titles in this miniseries, here's your chance to order them:

#521	BABY ON THE DOORSTEP	$3.50	☐
#526	DADDY TO THE RESCUE	$3.50	☐
#529	TOO MANY MOMS	$3.50	☐

TOTAL AMOUNT $
POSTAGE & HANDLING $
($1.00 for one book, 50¢ for each additional)
APPLICABLE TAXES* $_____
TOTAL PAYABLE $_____
(check or money order—please do not send cash)

To order, complete this form and send it, along with a check or money order for the total above, payable to Harlequin Books, to: *In the U.S.:* 3010 Walden Avenue, P.O. Box 9047, Buffalo, NY 14269-9047; *In Canada:* P.O. Box 613, Fort Erie, Ontario, L2A 5X3.

Name: _____
Address: _____ City: _____
State/Prov.: _____ Zip/Postal Code: _____

*New York residents remit applicable sales taxes.
Canadian residents remit applicable GST and provincial taxes.

DADS3

HARLEQUIN®

MARRIAGE By Design

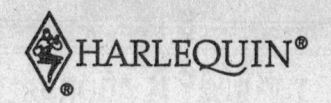

Harlequin proudly presents four stories about *convenient* but not *conventional* reasons for marriage:

- ◆ To save your godchildren from a "wicked stepmother"
- ◆ To help out your eccentric aunt—and her sexy business partner
- ◆ To bring an old man happiness by making him a grandfather
- ◆ To escape from a ghostly existence and become a real woman

Marriage By Design—four brand-new stories by four of Harlequin's most popular authors:

CATHY GILLEN THACKER
JASMINE CRESSWELL
GLENDA SANDERS
MARGARET CHITTENDEN

Don't miss this exciting collection of stories about marriages of convenience. Available in April, wherever Harlequin books are sold.

MBD94

This June, Harlequin invites you to a wedding of

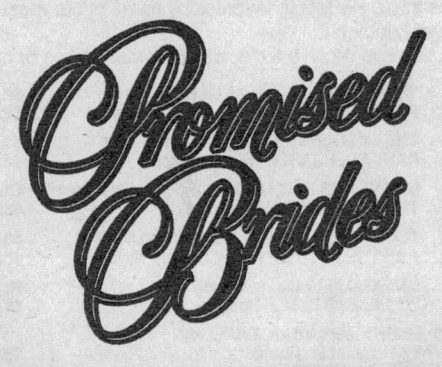

Promised Brides

Celebrate the joy and romance of weddings past with PROMISED BRIDES—a collection of original historical short stories, written by three best-selling historical authors:

> *The Wedding of the Century*—MARY JO PUTNEY
> *Jesse's Wife*—KRISTIN JAMES
> *The Handfast*—JULIE TETEL

Three unforgettable heroines, three award-winning authors! PROMISED BRIDES is available in June wherever Harlequin Books are sold.

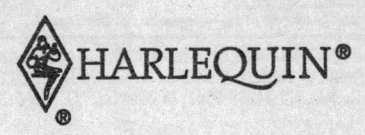

HARLEQUIN®

HARLEQUIN®

Don't miss these Harlequin favorites by some of our most distinguished authors!
And now, you can receive a discount by ordering two or more titles!

HT #25551	THE OTHER WOMAN by Candace Schuler	$2.99	☐
HT #25539	FOOLS RUSH IN by Vicki Lewis Thompson	$2.99	☐
HP #11550	THE GOLDEN GREEK by Sally Wentworth	$2.89	☐
HP #11603	PAST ALL REASON by Kay Thorpe	$2.99	☐
HR #03228	MEANT FOR EACH OTHER by Rebecca Winters	$2.89	☐
HR #03268	THE BAD PENNY by Susan Fox	$2.99	☐
HS #70532	TOUCH THE DAWN by Karen Young	$3.39	☐
HS #70540	FOR THE LOVE OF IVY by Barbara Kaye	$3.39	☐
HI #22177	MINDGAME by Laura Pender	$2.79	☐
HI #22214	TO DIE FOR by M.J. Rodgers	$2.89	☐
HAR #16421	HAPPY NEW YEAR, DARLING by Margaret St. George	$3.29	☐
HAR #16507	THE UNEXPECTED GROOM by Muriel Jensen	$3.50	☐
HH #28774	SPINDRIFT by Miranda Jarrett	$3.99	☐
HH #28782	SWEET SENSATIONS by Julie Tetel	$3.99	☐

Harlequin Promotional Titles

#83259	UNTAMED MAVERICK HEARTS (Short-story collection featuring Heather Graham Pozzessere, Patricia Potter, Joan Johnston)	$4.99	☐

(limited quantities available on certain titles)

	AMOUNT	$
DEDUCT:	10% DISCOUNT FOR 2+ BOOKS	$
	POSTAGE & HANDLING	$
	($1.00 for one book, 50¢ for each additional)	
	APPLICABLE TAXES*	$
	TOTAL PAYABLE	$
	(check or money order—please do not send cash)	

To order, complete this form and send it, along with a check or money order for the total above, payable to Harlequin Books, to: **In the U.S.:** 3010 Walden Avenue, P.O. Box 9047, Buffalo, NY 14269-9047; **In Canada:** P.O. Box 613, Fort Erie, Ontario, L2A 5X3.

Name: _____
Address: _____ City: _____
State/Prov.: _____ Zip/Postal Code: _____

*New York residents remit applicable sales taxes.
 Canadian residents remit applicable GST and provincial taxes.

HBACK-AJ